Karen Foley

HOT-BLOODED

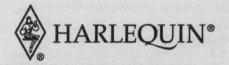

HARLEQUIN®

TORONTO • NEW YORK • LONDON
AMSTERDAM • PARIS • SYDNEY • HAMBURG
STOCKHOLM • ATHENS • TOKYO • MILAN • MADRID
PRAGUE • WARSAW • BUDAPEST • AUCKLAND

Recycling programs
for this product may
not exist in your area.

ISBN-13: 978-0-373-79567-3

HOT-BLOODED

Copyright © 2010 by Karen Foley.

"You've no regrets, then?"

Elena raised herself on her elbow to look at Chase. He lay against the pillows like a big, sleek cat. "I have absolutely no regrets. You've actually fulfilled a lifelong fantasy of mine."

He chuckled. "In that case, do you have any other fantasies you'd like me to fulfill? I'm here to serve."

"As a matter of fact..." she murmured, tracing his lower lip with her thumb, "there are a few more I'd like to explore."

Chase's eyes sharpened on her with interest. "Oh, yeah? Tell me."

Elena bit her lip, then leaned forward and whispered softly in his ear.

"Oh, God," Chase said with a soft groan, pulling her down so that she lay sprawled across him, her breasts flattened against his chest. "We have about five hours before dawn. I may die trying to do all those things, but I promise you, I'm going to go out a very happy man...."

Dear Reader,

I was so excited when my editor proposed the
It Takes a Hero series. What could be better than a
story that involves a tough, capable, totally hot guy
in a uniform? Especially when he's willing to put
everything—including his heart and his life—
on the line?

My day job with the Department of Defense provides
me with some unique opportunities to work alongside
our men and women in uniform, including those who
take voluntary deployments to Iraq and Afghanistan.
While I've never found the courage to do this myself,
several of my female colleagues have done so. For
the most part, these women have been assigned
to the larger bases with nice living quarters, fitness
centers, etc. But I couldn't help thinking...what
would happen if a woman suddenly found herself
in a remote outpost that contained none of these
amenities? What if she had to depend on a tough,
capable, irresistibly sexy guy for everything? And
what if he found himself tempted to throw protocol
and training out the window in order to meet her
every need?

I hope you enjoy Chase and Elena's story...and that it
meets *your* every reading need.

Enjoy!

Karen

ABOUT THE AUTHOR

Karen Foley is an incurable romantic. When she's not watching romantic movies, she's writing sexy romances with strong heroes and happy endings. She lives in Massachusetts with her husband and two daughters, and enjoys hearing from her readers. You can find out more about her by visiting www.karenefoley.com.

Books by Karen Foley

HARLEQUIN BLAZE
353—FLYBOY
422—OVERNIGHT SENSATION
451—ABLE-BODIED
504—HOLD ON TO THE NIGHTS

For my friends and colleagues, Storme, Greta,
Kelly, and Gladys—the fearless women
who have volunteered to serve and sacrifice.
You are amazing. Thank you for your support!

Prologue

Anbar Province, Iraq

THE SPIT of machine-gun fire and the acrid stench of burning oil and scorched metal filled the air. First Sergeant Chase McCormick surveyed the battle through a pair of high-optic binoculars from his perch atop an armored Humvee. He and his special ops team had just extracted a pair of Marine snipers from a site twenty miles away when they'd received reports of a large U.S. supply convoy traveling through the dangerous Anbar province. They'd immediately made a detour to intercept the convoy and escort them through the region, but they'd arrived too late.

Insurgents, hidden in an orchard on one side of the dusty road and in a crudely dug trench on the other, had attacked the convoy, which was now taking heavy fire from both sides. Chase had to give the truck drivers credit; along with their security detail, they were some tough sons of bitches and were holding their own.

Despite the fact the insurgents had managed to destroy two Humvees and the lead supply truck, their small-arms fire was mostly inaccurate and ineffectual. Chase had seen enough combat to know that this battle would be over shortly, but the entire scenario had him pissed off on a level so deep that he had to shut that part of himself down or risk losing his focus on the immediate mission.

While Al-Qaeda had, for the most part, been neutralized in the Anbar province, there were still pockets of rebellion and several attacks on the U.S. troops had occurred in recent weeks. Chase had received intel reports that the insurgents were hiding twenty miles to the north, where the sniper team had been conducting reconnaissance for the past five days. But in reality they had been here, digging their damned trenches and stockpiling their IEDs and rocket-propelled grenades.

As he watched, a driver exited one of the supply vehicles. Chase saw she was female, and she was aiming her weapon at the tree line, focused on some hidden target that even Chase couldn't see. In the next instant a second soldier, who up until that moment had been manning a fifty-caliber gun mounted on top of one of the convoy's gun trucks, abruptly abandoned his position and swung to the ground, apparently intent on intercepting and protecting the woman.

"Son of a bitch," Chase muttered beneath his breath, and swung his gun around to cover the man. Didn't he realize his best option for protecting the girl was to stay with his weapon?

As the soldier sprinted toward the woman, he took a direct hit from the assailant hidden in the trees, and went down on his knees before pitching face forward onto the ground. Chase swept the tree line with machine-gun fire, but was forced to stop when the female soldier stepped directly into his sights. She shouldered her weapon and bent to drag the wounded man to safety, and Chase reluctantly admired her guts even as he cursed her lack of self-preservation. She was completely vulnerable, and it seemed he was the only one who realized it.

Well, not the only one.

A shadow moved in the trees behind her, but before he could lock his sights on the target, the girl blocked his shot. Cursing, he shifted to a better position, when he saw the flash of a muzzle blast from the trees. The female soldier jerked once and then fell forward, covering the other soldier's body with her own and providing Chase with an unobstructed view of where the insurgent hid.

Only the man was no longer there.

Peering through the scope on his gun, Chase surveyed the area and saw the target lying in the grass beside a tree. He'd taken a direct hit, and Chase could see that he no longer posed a threat to anyone. He didn't need to guess who had eliminated the target; only the sniper team on the far ridge could have made such a difficult shot.

He swept his rifle scope over the two fallen soldiers to see that the female had risen to her knees. After briefly examining a wound to her shoulder, she bent over and began doggedly dragging her unconscious buddy across the ground to the relative safety of the trucks. Chase continued to provide cover, although he knew the sniper team was probably covering her, as well.

As much as he admired the woman for her bravery, Chase could have cheerfully shaken her. If she hadn't left the safety of her truck, then the gunner wouldn't have felt the need to abandon his own post in order to protect her, and neither of them would now be injured.

Women. He snorted in disgust.

He came from a long and distinguished line of military service, but there was one main reason he'd opted to join the Marine Corps special-operations command: they didn't allow females into their ranks.

He'd always maintained that women had no place in combat, an opinion that had less to do with their ability to do the job and more to do with the inability of their male counterparts to handle them doing the job. He'd seen hardened soldiers go soft and throw years of training and protocol out the window in order to protect a female soldier, or help her to complete a task that she could have handled on her own.

He had no idea if the gunner and the female soldier knew each other, but suspected there was some kind of romantic involvement. There usually was. The only thing worse than fighting alongside a female was fighting alongside one that you were also screwing, especially if you were fool enough to let it become about more than just sex. Nothing worse than letting a woman get under your skin.

The behavior he'd just witnessed only reinforced his belief that women shouldn't be placed in combat situations. He was convinced that if the female soldier had been a man, the gunner never would have abandoned his post. He'd have used his turret gun to cover her, the way he'd been trained to do.

Chase couldn't imagine losing control simply because a soldier was female. He prided himself on his ability to remain focused and make sound decisions, even under adverse conditions. If there was one thing he was sure of, it was that he'd never let a woman make him drop his guard on the battlefield. Or in the bedroom.

1

"IF YOU ASK ME, sex is overrated. I'll admit that it's pleasant, but earth-shattering? Not even close. Frankly, I don't know what all the fuss is about." Elena de la Vega arched a challenging eyebrow at her sister before taking a sip of her white wine.

"That's because you haven't had sex with the right guy," Carmen replied with a secretive gleam in her eyes. "Yet."

"Oh, c'mon," Elena scoffed, telling herself she didn't feel the tiniest bit jealous of the self-satisfied smile on Carmen's face. "Am I really supposed to believe that every time you and Nick get it on, he makes your toes curl with lust?"

Carmen set her martini down and leaned across the small table they shared, glancing quickly around to ensure none of the other patrons at the cozy sidewalk café could overhear their conversation. "Let's just say that Nick has a talent for making each time seem like the first time. You know, incredibly arousing. Exciting. Like I'm the hottest thing he's ever laid eyes on. The way he looks at me, and the things he does " Her expression took on a dreamy quality.

Elena rolled her eyes. "Yeah, well, I'll take your word for it. Nick may be great in bed, but he's also incredibly jealous. I couldn't be with a guy like that."

Carmen's smile grew wider. "Nick just wants other guys to know I'm with him. So what if he glowers a little bit, or likes to stay close to me when we're out together? At least he doesn't ignore me. I'm a happy, satisfied woman. Can you say the same?"

Elena thought of her own boyfriend, Larry, and a small sigh escaped her. He wasn't physically impressive, like Carmen's Nick was, but he was smart and considerate. They'd worked in the same office together for three years and Elena had a lot of respect for him. Larry was a conscientious man who took his job as a cost auditor for the Defense Procurement Agency seriously. He was brilliant when it came to numbers. Elena told herself again that she didn't mind if he worked long hours, or that he chose to spend most Saturdays in the office rather than with her. He treated her well, and when they did go out, he was a pleasant companion. Their typical routine was to catch a movie or a bite to eat, and then return to her apartment where he could be counted on to give her a very nice orgasm. Not an earth-shattering, body-clenching, toe-curling orgasm, but a nice one all the same.

"Larry is reliable," she finally said, but didn't meet her sister's knowing eyes. Instead, she trailed the tip of her finger around the edge of her wineglass. "I know what to expect with Larry. We get together on Wednesday and Saturday nights, and if our love life is a little…predictable, then who I am to complain?" She raised her gaze to Carmen's. "I actually prefer it that way."

"What way?" asked Carmen archly. "Flat on your back, making all the right noises so that he feels like a real man, while you just wish he'd hurry up and finish?"

Elena stared at her sister, amazed. "How did—? No, wait. It isn't like that."

"Isn't it? Don't forget, you're the one who dubbed him Old Faithful. As in…he's predictable and lasts less than two minutes."

Elena groaned and took a hefty swig of her wine. "That's not fair. I was a little tipsy that night and said more than I should have. You're taking it out of context. I dubbed him Old Faithful because he's, well, dependable. Trustworthy. *Faithful.* All good traits for a man to have."

"Or a dog," Carmen muttered. Then, seeing Elena's expression, she was instantly contrite. "I agree with you. Absolutely. Those are all good qualities for a man to have, but they shouldn't be his only qualities. He should make your insides turn to mush and your pulse quicken just thinking about him." Her expression grew earnest. "Please tell me you're not going to marry this guy, Elena. You deserve so much more. Every woman should have one great passion in her life. Don't settle for mediocrity."

"He hasn't asked me to marry him yet," Elena grumbled. "And I said our love life is predictable, not mediocre."

"Oh, come on," Carmen scoffed, and sat back in her chair. "Your boyfriend is boring. Your *life* is boring. When was the last time you did something exciting?

Something that made your heart pound and your mouth go dry?" She leaned forward again. "You're almost thirty, Elena, and yet you've never done any of the wacky things that most people do when they're in their twenties. Nick and I had sex on the roof of his building last night, under the stars. It was amazing."

"Nick's rooftop garden is amazing," Elena said drily, ignoring her sister's jabs. "I'm sure you're not the first girl he's brought up there."

Carmen narrowed her eyes. "So what if I'm not the first? I'll be the last."

Elena shrugged. "Well, it's your heart. Risk it if you want to."

"See? That's my whole point. You're not willing to take any risks, Elena. You'd rather settle for safe and boring than take a chance on something exciting. Something that could change your life." She shook her head in mock sadness. "You have no idea what you're missing."

Elena dabbed her mouth with her linen napkin before folding it neatly beside her plate, silently counting to ten. She refused to be baited.

"I don't feel as if I'm settling," she finally said, hoping that she sounded convincing. "And not everyone wants that kind of excitement in their life, Carmen. I've watched what great passion has done to Mom and Dad, and even to you." She fished in her pocketbook for some money and carefully placed several bills on the table. "I don't want that kind of chaos in my life. Larry is kind and considerate and I always know exactly what to expect from him. I'm happy with what I have." Seeing the disbelief on her sister's face, she stood up. "Really, I am. Look, I have to go. Thanks for lunch. I'll call you tomorrow."

As she walked to her car, Elena refused to feel guilty for prematurely ending their lunch. The whole thing was Carmen's fault, anyway. It seemed every time they got together, the conversation turned to Elena's love life. Neither of her two sisters could understand Larry's appeal, but they didn't know him the way Elena did. Admittedly, he wasn't adventurous in bed, but so what? Not everyone was into *that kinky stuff,* as Larry put it. And any therapist worth his salt would tell you that a successful relationship should be based on trust and mutual respect. Not sex.

Never sex.

All she had to do was look at her family for proof. Given the choice between a life of calm predictability or the blood-pounding, roof-raising drama that seemed to accompany her parents and her siblings wherever they went, Elena preferred the former.

She always would.

Even so, her sister's words rankled, partly because Elena knew that on some level, they were true. But she'd chosen her path with careful deliberation. Sure, there were times when she felt that she was meant for something bigger and more exciting, but she simply had to spend time with her parents and sisters to remember exactly why she'd opted for the conventional life she now led.

Her family might boast about the hot, Spanish blood that flowed through their veins, claiming it was the reason for their unpredictable and often volatile behavior, but Elena wanted no part of it. She'd watched her parents divorce and remarry each other twice; she'd spent countless nights with each of her sisters, lending both an ear and a shoulder as they'd wept and wailed about the failure of yet another relationship. Her younger sister, Sarita, actually enjoyed dating two, even three men at a time and then watching the fireworks when they found out about each other. That kind of excitement she could do without.

Granted, Nick Belcastro seemed like a decent guy, and he was both gorgeous and financially independent, but Elena wondered how long he'd tolerate Carmen's mood swings before he decided he'd had enough.

Elena glanced at her watch as she pulled out of the restaurant parking lot. Nearly one-thirty. Was Larry still at the office? They had plans to go out to dinner and a movie later on, but Elena suddenly had an urge to see him, if only to reassure herself that he wasn't as mediocre as Carmen claimed. She could picture him in his office, surrounded by papers, with his hair sticking up from where he'd combed his fingers through it in frustration. Deciding he could use a break, she swung the car in the direction of the federal building where they both worked. Even if he'd already left, there was some paperwork she could collect from her own office and bring home with her.

Twenty minutes later, Elena passed through the security checkpoint and walked through the darkened corridors toward Larry's office. The Defense Procurement Agency oversaw the purchase and delivery of goods and services for the military. Elena and Larry worked in the agency's headquarters, an impressive four-story structure of limestone and sleek marble, located on the outskirts of Washington, D.C.

After obtaining her law degree, Elena had spent the first few years of her career negotiating and administering contracts for the military, everything from nuts and bolts to major weapons systems. She was good at what she did. So good that she'd been offered a promotion to the DPA's legal department, writing policy and procedure manuals for the agency's contracting center. There was very little that Elena didn't know about contracting, both from an administrative and a legal perspective.

Her parents might be disappointed that she hadn't chosen to use her law degree in litigation, but striding up and down a courtroom while making impassioned speeches to a judge and jury held little appeal for Elena. Nope, she enjoyed researching regulations and statutes, and then applying them to how the agency did business. She didn't mind sitting through oversight meetings and briefing senior leadership on changes in federal procurement policy. She told herself yet again that what she did mattered. She was making a difference.

Elena stopped briefly at the mailroom and checked her box, flipping through the assorted envelopes and papers for anything that might require her immediate attention. Most of the mail was routine correspondence, including a letter from the Director's office requesting civilian volunteers—especially those with contracts and legal experience—to work in Iraq for six months, negotiating and monitoring the defense contracts there. According to the memo, such volunteer deployments were the agency's number-one mission.

Elena snorted. As if *that* would ever happen. This was the third such call for volunteers in as many months, and while most folks who did volunteer had only positive things to say about their deployment experience, Elena couldn't imagine working in Iraq or Afghanistan. While she had an extensive background negotiating military contracts, the agency couldn't pay her enough money to go over there. She disliked being hot, and having mortars lobbed at her wasn't a huge incentive, either.

Carrying her mail in one hand, she walked toward Larry's office. His door was closed and she had a moment's regret that she'd missed him, when she saw a shadow pass beneath the crack at the bottom. Just then, a crash sounded from behind the closed door and Elena heard Larry give a pained groan.

"Larry!" She thrust the door open so hard that it slammed against the wall, and then she stood there, speechless at the sight that greeted her.

Larry stood at the side of his desk with his pants and underwear crumpled around his ankles, his shirt open and flapping loosely around his pale buttocks and thighs. Sprawled facedown across his desk was a woman, her black skirt pushed up around her waist. Her legs were splayed wide, the stiletto heels on her shoes lending them extra length. Larry gripped the woman's hips as she bent forward over the desk, thrusting himself into her. His head was thrown back and the cords in his neck stood out in a way that Elena had never seen when he'd been with *her.*

The crash she'd heard had been Larry's alabaster paperweight falling to the floor as the woman swept it from the surface of the desk in her frenzy. The paperweight Elena had given to him on Valentine's Day last year.

In the instant before they both turned toward her, Elena recognized the other woman as one of the new interns they'd hired in the legal department. Her reddish hair fell forward over her face, and her eyes were hazy with pleasure. Her full lips were parted and moist as she gripped the edges of the desk and arched her back to give Larry better access. When she raised herself to look toward the door, Elena saw her pink blouse was open at the front and her bra was pulled down below her breasts, which had left a damp mark on the glossy veneer of the desk.

For a moment, the three of them stared at each other. Larry's harsh breathing was the only sound that broke the stunned silence, until he muttered an oath and snatched himself from the woman's body.

Elena didn't wait to see more. She turned on her heel and walked blindly back the way she'd come, unable to dispel the erotic images she'd just witnessed. She tried to recall when the woman—Claire—had first begun working at the agency. Five months ago, maybe? Six? How long had she and Larry been having an affair? Was this what he did every Saturday when he told her he was going into the office?

"Elena, *wait.*"

Larry trotted down the corridor after her, shoving his shirt into his waistband. Elena stopped and watched him approach, noting his flushed features and disheveled hair. She'd always thought he was attractive, but now all she could see were his white legs and thin buttocks, pumping furiously into another woman.

"What do you want, Larry?" She glanced at her watch, ignoring how her hand trembled. "I really can't stay. I only came by because I thought you needed a break from work." She gave a bitter laugh. "Little did I know."

Larry swiped a hand through his hair, looking both embarrassed and defiant. "You should have called. You always call first."

Elena gaped at him. "I should have *called?* Excuse me, but I work here, too. I don't need your permission to come by the office after hours, Larry." She ran a scathing eye over him. "It figures that the first time I do, this is what I find. You, in a sweaty clutch with the office intern. It's so cliché that it's actually pathetic. What if someone else had seen you? You both could be fired for this."

"I think I'm in love with her," he blurted, then swiped a hand across his face. "I mean, I know I'm in love with her. I *am* in love with her."

Elena's mouth fell open, but no words came out. She stared at him, speechless.

"I'm sorry," he muttered, clearly uncomfortable. "I didn't mean for you to find us—to find out like this." He rubbed the back of his neck and glanced toward his office where he'd left Claire. "It's just that—"

"What?" Elena asked sarcastically. "I wasn't willing to spread myself across your desk? To fulfill your naughty little fantasies? Maybe I would have done it, Larry. Maybe all you had to do was ask, but now you'll never know what I might have done, will you?"

To Elena's dismay, Larry's face grew tight. "I never asked, because I already knew what the answer would be. You're not exactly Miss Excitement."

"What is that supposed to mean?" Elena gasped, but she had a sinking feeling that she already knew. His words sounded a little too much like the conversation she'd had with her sister earlier that day.

"I don't want to hurt you more than I already have," Larry began, "but it wasn't until I met Claire that I realized what I'd been missing with you."

Elena's eyebrows flew up. *What?* The numbness that had enveloped her when she'd first walked into Larry's office was rapidly vanishing, to be replaced with a slow, simmering anger.

"Oh, and what would that be?" she asked sweetly. "I don't seem to recall that you were missing out on anything. You had sex every week—and that was just with me. I always paid my own way when we went out. I never objected if you wanted to play golf with the guys, or head up to Atlantic City for a weekend. I never demanded anything of you, Larry, and I was always there when you wanted me. Basically, you had a perfect relationship."

Larry missed the sharp edge beneath the silken veil of her words. "Yeah, it was a perfect relationship all right. Perfectly boring."

"Boring? You think I'm boring?"

Larry made a sound of frustration. "No, that's not what I said, but since you brought it up, then yes! I think you're boring. Okay? Are you happy now? I said it!"

"Oh. My. God." Elena stared at him in disbelief. "You're serious."

Didn't he realize that in their relationship *he* was the boring one? He was the stereotypical accountant—detailed, meticulous and not given to extravagance or grand gestures. He was the kind of guy that you'd pass on the street and never look at twice. He appealed to her because he was ordinary and because she always knew what to expect from him. At least, she amended silently, she'd thought she always knew what to expect. And now, to find out that he thought *she* was boring!

"Listen, Elena, you're a beautiful woman, but you're too set in your ways. You need to be a little more flexible. You need to live a little."

Elena arched an eyebrow. "It certainly appears your

new girlfriend is flexible. Is that what this is all about, Larry? Having sex in forbidden places?"

Larry's face turned a ruddy shade. "No, of course not. But it does have something to do with spontaneity. Face it, Elena. Your entire life is about order and routine. You're a creature of habit, and you hate surprises. You're about as capable of spontaneity as a fish is of flying."

Later, Elena would not be sure what made her do it. She only knew that in that particular moment, the most important thing in the world was to prove Larry wrong. To show him irrefutable proof that she was as capable of being spontaneous and exciting as the next person. She snatched the director's memorandum from the sheaf of mail she clutched in her hand and waved it beneath Larry's nose.

"Oh, yeah? Well, here's a little bit of spontaneity for you. I've decided to do a six-month deployment to Iraq."

To her dismay, Larry's eyebrows flew up, and he gave a snort of disbelieving laughter. "Oh, come on. We both know you're bluffing. When did you decide this? Two seconds ago? We both know you'd never volunteer to go over there. You may not be a spur-of-the-moment girl, but you're not stupid, either. Besides, you enjoy your creature comforts just a little too much to go to Iraq for six months. I can't picture you sharing a B-hut with twenty other women, or eating in a chow hall every night."

"Oh, really?" Elena tossed her head. "Well, believe it or not, I'm going. And I understand there are battalions of healthy, young, hard-bodied soldiers who would do *anything* to keep me safe. In fact, I'm sure my deployment will be rewarding on many different levels."

To her satisfaction, Larry no longer looked quite so skeptical. "You're kidding, right? That's your damned sisters talking. You'd never actually do it."

Elena gave him a sweet smile. "Watch me," she purred, and turned on her heel and walked away.

2

Kuwait City, six weeks later

THWAP, THWAP, thwap.

The steady sound of helicopter blades cut through the air overhead, but Elena hardly noticed the noise. After three days spent sitting in a converted hangar alongside the U.S. military airstrip in Kuwait City, she'd become well accustomed to the sound of both helicopters and jets as they came in and then left again. The kicker was she should have been on one of those helicopters long before now.

She'd seen her orders; she was going to the Green Zone in Baghdad, where she would try to clean up the colossal mess that had been made of the military contracts there. She'd heard countless stories about how good the quality of life was in the Zone, and she'd actually begun looking forward to her deployment. In the six weeks since she'd volunteered to come to Iraq, she'd had plenty of opportunity to examine her life and had concluded that both Carmen and Larry were right—it was boring.

But that was all about to change. She was shaking things up in a big way. She'd embarked on an adventure and made a promise to herself to embrace each new and exciting opportunity as it came her way, no matter what. Now she stared at the woman holding the clipboard that contained her new orders, and silently counted to ten, willing herself to control her rising temper.

"What do you mean they've changed my assignment?" she demanded in dismay. "I've been sitting in this hangar for three days, waiting for a sandstorm to subside so that I can fly to Baghdad, Iraq. As in the Green Zone, complete with fitness center, modern plumbing and a fast-food burger joint. That's what I signed up for—" she broke off to glance at the front of the woman's uniform "—Major Dumfries. Not some remote outpost in northern Afghanistan."

The other woman didn't even have the grace to look apologetic. Instead, she met Elena's gaze unflinchingly. "Your deployment paperwork clearly states that your assignment can change at any time, depending on need. The Defense Procurement Agency has indicated they now need you in Afghanistan, and *you* need to be flexible, ma'am." She glanced again at the clipboard. "We have a helicopter departing for the outpost at 0600 hours tomorrow morning. I'll see you back here at the airstrip then."

Elena's mouth fell open. "Wait! That's it? Just like that, I'm now going to some hellhole in Afghanistan? How can you do this? Is it even legal?"

Major Dumfries smiled. "I don't make the assignments, ma'am. I just make sure the folks get there in one piece."

Elena took a deep breath and reminded herself yet

again that this was an adventure—a new opportunity—
and she would embrace it wholeheartedly. She pasted a
smile on her face.

"Fine. I'll go to this outpost." Reaching down, she
lifted her rucksack onto one shoulder and then hefted
her two duffel bags with as much dignity as she could
manage, considering they weighed about a gazillion
pounds each. She started to turn away, and then swung
back toward the Major. "Just out of curiosity, what kind
of facilities do they have at this place?"

"Facilities?" The other woman's eyebrow arched.

"Yes. As in dining hall, fitness center, recreation center…please tell me this outpost has *facilities*."

Major Dumfries's mouth twitched. "I understand
they're still in the process of improving the post, but
they do have toilets and showers."

Elena stared at her. "What about a dining hall? They
must have that, right?"

"I believe there is a dining facility, yes."

Elena drew in a deep breath. "Are there any other
civilians at this outpost?"

"Several, as a matter of fact."

Elena supposed she should be grateful for that. If
there were other civilians at the outpost, then the living
conditions couldn't be too primitive. But she'd heard
horror stories about some of the forward operating bases
located on the northern and eastern perimeters of Afghanistan, particularly in regards to their vulnerability.
She hadn't planned on going to an area that was poten-
tially dangerous. After all, she wasn't a soldier. She had
no combat training. She was a contracts geek—a desk
jockey, for Pete's sake. Her job was to meet with the
defense contractors who were doing work on the various

military bases and to negotiate terms and conditions for performance of that work. Aside from ensuring that the soldiers had the facilities and equipment they needed to perform their jobs, she had no military background.

"I've heard some of these outlying bases come under frequent attack by the Taliban," she ventured. "Is that the case with this particular base?"

Major Dumfries gave her a reassuring smile. "You'll be in safe hands, ma'am. We haven't lost a civilian yet. There's a special-operations detachment based there. They'll keep you safe."

Elena swiped a hand across her eyes. "I need a drink."

She wasn't aware she'd muttered the words aloud until she saw the amusement in the other woman's eyes. "Alcohol is prohibited in Kuwait City, ma'am."

"Great," she replied. "I can't even have a last drink before I leave civilization."

Major Dumfries tucked the clipboard under her arm and leaned forward, glancing around to ensure they wouldn't be overheard. "This is strictly off the record, but sometimes the U.S. embassy personnel have access to alcohol. I understand they're having a small send-off tonight over at the hotel for some of their aides who are returning to the States."

A party? At the hotel? That was the first positive bit of news she'd had since arriving in Kuwait City three days earlier. Since then, it seemed she'd done nothing but schlep her gear back and forth between the hotel and the military airstrip, waiting for transportation to her final destination. Which was supposed to be the Green Zone, not some scary outpost in eastern Afghanistan.

Oh, yeah, she definitely needed a drink.

"Do I need an invitation to get in?"

"No, ma'am. Just take the elevator up to the concierge level at 2000 hours and follow the noise. Nobody will even notice you're there. But don't overdo it. The only thing worse than flying in a helicopter is flying in one with a hangover."

ELENA STEPPED OUT of the elevator and paused. Major Dumfries had been right about the noise; she could hear the festivities from down the hall, and it sounded as if the party was in full swing. She hesitated, hoping she'd dressed appropriately. Nothing worse than standing out in a crowd when all she wanted to do was blend in. While she'd brought five sets of agency-issued uniforms with her, she'd been restricted on how much civilian clothing she could bring from home, and had settled on several pairs of pants and tops, and some comfortable workout gear. The crimson blouse she'd chosen to wear with her jeans wasn't dressy, but it would have to do. She wore her dark hair loose around her shoulders, allowing it to wave naturally around her face, and had opted for just a touch of mascara and some lipstick.

She drew in a deep breath and smoothed her palms over the seat of her jeans. Crashing a party of strangers was totally out of character for her, not to mention bad manners. She wasn't sure she had the courage to go through with it.

But then she remembered that by this time tomorrow, she'd be hundreds of miles away from here and nobody would even remember—or care—that she'd been at this party. She'd never even see these people again. Really, what did she have to lose? This might be the last night she had to enjoy herself for the next six months.

Straightening her spine, she followed the sound of music and laughter. If this was going to be her last night in civilization, she was going to make it one to remember.

As soon as she stepped into the function room, Elena realized she needn't have worried. There were dozens of people inside, all of them talking or laughing together in small groups, and none of them paid her any attention. Several even smiled at her in a friendly, offhand manner. The lights had been dimmed to a pleasant glow, and a bar had been set up along one wall. The music was loud and upbeat, and a cloud of cigarette smoke hung suspended near the ceiling. Most of the people were men of varying ages and although all of them wore casual clothing, it wasn't difficult for Elena to distinguish the active-duty military from the civilians. If their haircuts didn't set them apart, their physical conditioning did.

Elena skirted the crowd and sidled over to the bar, where bottles of alcohol were lined up alongside plastic cups and an ice bucket. When she didn't see a bartender, she looked around, uncertain.

"It's an open bar, hon, so help yourself."

Elena turned to see a woman approach the bar beside her and liberally pour herself a glass of white wine from an uncorked bottle. She was older than Elena, probably in her forties.

"Are you sure? I mean, who provided all of this?"

The woman smiled and gave Elena a friendly wink. "You know the old adage—don't ask, don't tell. All I can say is drink up, because you never know when we'll have this opportunity again."

That was the truth, Elena thought bleakly. Just thinking about what lay in store for her in the days and weeks ahead made her unaccountably homesick for her cozy little apartment back home. Despite the fact that she'd volunteered for this deployment, right now she couldn't think of a single good reason for being here. Most people who volunteered did so because they had some patriotic calling or felt the need to support the troops in some way. Others did it for the money, which was in itself a huge incentive. But not her.

Nope.

She'd come because she'd had something to prove. Because she'd wanted everyone—her sister and cheating ex-boyfriend included—to see that she could be spontaneous and adventurous. She'd wanted to kick-start her life back into gear, but right now she just felt out of place and oddly alone, even in the midst of the party. She'd been excited about going to Baghdad, knowing she'd be just one of hundreds of civilians, and that the quality of life there was pretty good. But the prospect of spending six months at a remote outpost in the wilds of Afghanistan was another matter altogether. Quite frankly, it scared the hell out of her. She recalled Major Dumfries' assurance that they hadn't lost a civilian yet, but found little comfort in her words.

"I haven't seen you around before," the woman continued. "Where are you stationed?"

"Oh, I just came in from the States three days ago," Elena explained. "I've been waiting for transportation to Baghdad, but just found out this morning that my orders have been changed."

The woman nodded sympathetically. "That happens a lot. Where are they sending you now?"

Elena squinted, trying to recall the name of the base where she was headed. "Some forward operating base in Afghanistan. Shangri-la?" She laughed. "No, that's not right, because I'm pretty sure this place isn't paradise."

"Do you mean *Sharlana?*"

"Yes! That's the place."

The woman's face grew sober, and she took a long swallow of her wine, avoiding eye contact.

"What's wrong?" Elena asked, dread uncoiling in her stomach. "Do you know something about Shangri-la that I don't?"

The woman lowered her cup and sighed. "Didn't you hear? The Taliban attacked a U.S. base just forty miles north of Sharlana last night. Eight civilians were killed."

What?

Elena stared at the woman. "Are you sure?"

"Oh, yeah." The woman gave a bitter laugh. "There are no military stationed there. Rumor has it that the civilians who were assigned there—including the ones who died—had ties to the CIA, so the base is probably only used by intelligence personnel."

Elena blew out a hard breath. "That's awful." She hesitated. "Has anything like that ever happened at Shangri-la, er, Sharlana?"

"Not that I know of, but then again, there's a Marine expeditionary unit stationed at Sharlana to deter any attacks." She smiled at Elena. "You'll be perfectly safe."

That was the second time that day she'd heard those words, so why did she have trouble believing them? With a groan, she grabbed the nearest bottle and proceeded to pour several fingers of a pale green liquor into a plastic cup. She tipped it back, swallowing the entire contents in a single, long gulp and then gasped as the alcohol burned the back of her throat and made her eyes sting.

"Whoa, take it easy," admonished the other woman, watching her with a mixture of astonishment and admiration. "That stuff'll knock you on your ass."

"Oh, good," Elena gasped, as warmth seeped through her body. "I'm actually in need of a little technical knockout."

The woman laughed. "Suit yourself. Just remember that you've been warned. Good luck, hon."

Elena watched the woman saunter away before she poured herself another glass of the green liquid, this time filling the cup. The alcohol had left a pleasant taste in her mouth, a sweet mixture of black licorice with minty undertones. She took a hefty swig, swirling the liquid around on her tongue and enjoying the flavor. She never drank anything other than wine or the occasional glass of beer, and now she wondered why. This stuff was delicious.

"Careful there. You know what they say about the Green Devil."

The voice was deep and amused, and something inside Elena quivered in response. She turned to see a man leaning negligently against the bar, watching her. A broad-shouldered, lean-hipped man with a face that could have graced any number of different magazines, from guns and hunting, to high fashion. The appreciation in his eyes, combined with his lazy smile, caused a rush of heat to slide through her veins that had nothing to do with the liquor she'd just consumed.

He wore a black T-shirt and jeans, and her first thought was that he had a body designed for battle—or a woman's pleasure—honed to masculine perfection and sculpted in a way that she'd read about but had never actually seen up close. He had impossibly chiseled cheekbones and a mouth that would put a Renaissance angel to shame. In the indistinct light, she couldn't tell what color his eyes were, and his dark hair was cropped close in a distinctly military style. He was altogether delicious.

Elena wanted to bite him.

The thought came out of nowhere and shocked her so much that she started, sloshing the alcohol over her fingers.

"Green Devil?" she repeated lamely, sucking the liquid from her fingers and trying not to stare.

He nodded toward the cup she held. "Another name for absinthe." Reaching out, his hand closed around the cup, his fingers brushing against hers and sending a quicksilver thrill of awareness through her. "Did you know this stuff was banned in the U.S. until just a few years ago?"

"No, I had no idea." Elena watched as he swirled the cup in contemplation. "Why was it banned?"

He raised his gaze to hers, and one corner of his delectable mouth lifted in the barest hint of a smile. "The government believed it contained hallucinogenic properties, and could cause a person to lose their sanity."

Elena had absolutely no doubt that it was true. In fact, she was certain that she was hallucinating at that exact instant. What other reason could there be for the vivid images that were flying through her head? Images of this man, naked and gleaming with sweat as his body moved with purpose and strength over hers, his muscles flexing as he drove into her. She could actually *smell* him, a mixture of pure, male sex and something subtle and spicy, and the combination made her feel intoxicated.

Oh, yeah. She had definitely lost her sanity.

She passed a hand over her eyes and gave a shaky

laugh, trying to dispel the erotic imagery. "Wow. I had no idea. I guess I owe you a big thank-you for saving me."

"Chase McCormick," he said, extending a hand. "Always glad to be of service."

Oh, if only!

Elena reached out, and his fingers closed warmly over hers. Hardly realizing she did so, she stepped closer to him. The only thing she was conscious of was a slow heat building low in her abdomen, and how her breasts felt full and tight.

"Elena de la Vega." Was that her voice that sounded so husky and breathless?

He smiled, and the floor shifted beneath Elena's feet. The man was more gorgeous than he had any right to be, but when he smiled...sweet mercy!

"Easy," he said, and set the cup aside to grasp her beneath her elbow. He dipped his head to look into her eyes. "You okay? For a second there, you looked as if you were going down."

Now *there* was an idea.

How long had it been since she'd pleasured a man with her mouth? On that score, her sister Carmen had been right. Her sex life *had* been boring and predictable, and as much as she'd like to put the blame fully on Larry, he'd had no trouble trying something risqué with his new girlfriend. Which meant Elena must be the one with the problem, and it was way past time she did something about it.

Now she looked at Chase McCormick, and just the thought of tasting him...of having him in her mouth... caused ribbons of lust to unfurl low in her belly. In fact, just thinking about touching this man caused her heart to beat faster. She had no idea who this guy was, and yet here she was, contemplating doing risqué things with him that she'd never done with Larry.

Her eyes slid over Chase again, admiring the broad thrust of his shoulders and the way his T-shirt hugged the contours of his pecs and his flat stomach. She wanted badly to touch him.

She'd worked with dozens of military guys over the years, and while several of them had made their interest in her clear, Elena had never been tempted into a relationship. For the most part, they'd been too masculine, brimming with testosterone and confidence. She'd known instinctively that a man like that could overwhelm her, both physically and emotionally. The last thing she needed—or wanted—was to be dependent on another person for her own happiness. She'd seen what that kind of neediness had done to her parents and had vowed she wouldn't make the same mistake.

But as her gaze drifted over Chase's leanly muscled physique, she couldn't help but wonder what it might be like to be with him, to let him overwhelm her.

To lose herself in him.

He was the sort who would take his time with a woman, ensuring her pleasure before reaching his own. He would be assertive, playful and maybe even a little kinky. For one wild instant, her imagination surged. Images of Chase, wearing nothing but his dog tags, played through her head as she envisioned all the things they could do.

Then she remembered that after tonight, she would leave for some godforsaken outpost in northern Afghanistan where there was a real possibility, however small, that she would be killed. In that instant, she regretted every wild, crazy, impetuous thing she had never done. For instance, she'd never had casual sex, and had never engaged in a one-night stand. Instead, she'd deluded herself into believing she was happy having mediocre sex with Larry Gorman.

But she still had tonight to make up for all those years of self-denial, and somehow she had a feeling that this guy could make it all worthwhile. Withdrawing her hand from Chase's, Elena deliberately picked up the cup of absinthe.

"I'm fine," she assured him, smiling. "In fact, I'm better than fine, and if this stuff makes a person insane, then I want more." Without taking her eyes from his, she tipped the cup back and drained the contents, willing herself not to cough on the strong alcohol. When she'd swallowed it, she delicately licked her lips and gave him what she hoped was a seductive look. "Because tonight, I intend to go a little crazy. Wanna come along for the ride?"

3

CHASE SWEPT HIS GAZE over the woman, trying not to let his surprise show, trying not to let her see how much he wanted to accept her offer. She'd caught his attention the moment she'd walked through the door, alone and looking a little apprehensive. He was certain she didn't work at the embassy; she lacked the self-important swagger so common among the State Department personnel. That meant she was a Department of Defense civilian or a contractor, either just coming into the Middle Eastern theater or leaving it. He hoped like hell it was the latter.

She appealed to him on a primal level, from her lustrous dark hair and suggestive smile, to her full breasts and shapely ass. He wanted to do things with her that he had no business doing, not when he was leaving for a yearlong deployment. What could he offer her, or any woman for that matter, beyond a single night? Then again, if he were to take her proposition seriously, it seemed that was all she was interested in. A single night.

The prospect was tempting. More than tempting,

especially considering he was looking down the loaded gun barrel of enforced celibacy. Twelve long months of it. Even if the military lifted the ban on sex during deployments, he wouldn't be doing the horizontal tango with anyone. Females in uniform were off-limits, end of discussion.

But this particular female was something altogether different. He'd stake his life on the fact that she wasn't in the military, so technically he wasn't prohibited from getting involved with her. Besides, he was more or less off duty until dawn, when he'd board an Apache helicopter and fly to the forward operating base that he'd call home for the next twelve months.

"Dance with me," he commanded softly and caught her hand, pulling her toward him.

She came willingly into his arms, and he slid one hand to the small of her back, holding her just close enough that he could feel the heat emanating from her body and smell the fragrance of her hair. There was no dance floor, so he simply swayed with her where they stood, enjoying the sensation of just holding a woman in his arms. Of holding this woman. Her breath fanned his neck, and he had to resist the urge to pull her even closer. Her scent filled his head and made him want to bend her over his arm and bury his face against her skin.

"Well, this is nice," she drawled, tipping her head back to smile at him, "but not quite what I had in mind." Her voice was rich with suggestion. As if to emphasize her meaning, she sidled closer, so that her breasts pressed against his chest.

Chase's body responded instantly to her nearness, tightening until he was uncomfortably aware of his own arousal pressing against the zipper of his jeans.

day Chase had been accepted into MARSOC, the elite Marine Corps Special Operations Command.

He'd redeployed back to Camp Lejeune six months ago after spending a year in Iraq, and had been glad for the opportunity to spend some time with his parents and sisters. But when his team had been called up to Afghanistan, he'd been happy to go. Too much time in the States made him feel as if he was going soft.

They reached her floor, and now Chase guided her out of the elevator with one hand at the small of her back. He could have simply let her find her own way, but told himself that he had an obligation to see her safely to her room. He also knew he was full of shit. He simply wasn't ready to say goodbye to this woman.

They came to her room much too quickly.

"Here you go," he said gruffly. He inserted her key into the door, pushing it open for her and then stepping back.

Away from temptation.

She didn't go in. Instead, she leaned against the door frame and considered him. The silky fabric of her blouse stretched taut across her breasts, emphasizing the thrust of her nipples. Chase swallowed hard. He could easily spend hours exploring her lush curves, but it was the expression in her eyes that made it impossible for him to move away. She was looking at him as if he were the most desirable man she'd ever seen, and his own body pulsed hotly in response.

"I wish I wasn't leaving tomorrow," she finally said. "I'd have liked to get to know you better."

Chase gave her a rueful smile, feeling her regret. "Just bad timing, I guess."

She laughed softly. "You're not kidding. I'm the queen

of bad timing." She glanced into the open room and then back at Chase, and he knew what was coming before she said the words. "We could get to know each other tonight…if you want to. It's still early."

Chase blew out a hard breath and rubbed a hand across the back of his neck, hoping she didn't see his body's instant response to her words. Visions of her, lying across the sheets, her skin warm and smooth, filled his head. His cock swelled as he imagined himself filling his hands with her breasts, kissing her softness. Did he want to stay? Hell, yes. The problem was, he knew he wouldn't want to leave, and he had an 0430 bird to catch.

"Forget it," she said quickly, misinterpreting his gesture. She crossed her arms defensively around her middle and gave him an overly bright smile. "Not such a great idea, I get it."

"No," he said roughly, stepping toward her. "That's not it at all."

He had a thing about honesty, sometimes to his own detriment. The only time he lied was when he absolutely had to, like when he was on a mission. Then, he could lie so beautifully that his own mother wouldn't doubt he'd told the truth. And he had no problem with small white lies if they were harmless, like telling a woman that no, those pants did not make her ass look big. But he had a sinking feeling that now was going to be one of those times when he'd look back and regret his own inability to completely dupe a woman. It was important to him that she understand his reasons for turning her down.

"You're a beautiful woman," he continued. "Being with you tonight would be…amazing, but it couldn't be anything more than just one night. I leave at dawn for a twelve-month deployment, so anything more would be impossible. I wouldn't want either of us to have regrets about it tomorrow. Especially when one of us has had too much to drink."

She pushed herself away from the doorjamb, and Chase could see the resignation and regret in her luminous eyes.

"I understand, and I think you're really sweet." She smiled at him. "Leave it to me to find the one guy in the world with scruples."

Scruples he'd rather do without, Chase thought grimly. He had to be the biggest idiot on the face of the planet to turn down what she was offering, but he knew from experience that casual sex never made him feel better, either about himself or the woman involved. Nope, better to let her go now and keep his fantasies about whatever might have been.

"Nobody has ever described me as sweet," he said sardonically, to cover his own conflicting emotions. "If any of my men overheard you say that, you'd completely destroy my reputation as a hard-ass."

"It will be our secret," Elena promised, "so please don't change." Standing on tiptoe, she pressed a kiss against his cheek. At least, Chase suspected the kiss was meant for his cheek, but he instinctively turned his head to follow her movement, bringing his lips into direct contact with hers.

She stilled for a moment, and Chase realized his hands were resting loosely at her waist, while hers were pressed lightly against his chest for balance.

"I'm sorry," she breathed, just before she pressed her mouth fully against his.

FOR AN INSTANT, Elena thought he would either pull back or push her away. He held himself so rigidly still that if it weren't for the warmth of his lips beneath hers, he might have been carved from stone. Elena knew she'd had too much to drink, but she hadn't consumed so much that she didn't know exactly what she was doing. The alcohol only blunted the sharp edges of her self-restraint and allowed her to loosen her tightly laced inhibitions. When he didn't immediately move to end the kiss, Elena softened it, shaping the contours of his beautiful mouth.

A shudder went through him, and he made a sound like a half groan. Emboldened, Elena slid her hands along his rib cage and angled her mouth ever so slightly across his, enjoying the sensuality of the kiss. There was something erotic about being the aggressor, especially when she knew Chase could easily overpower her.

He didn't resist when she backed him up against the open door of her room and delicately stroked her tongue along the seam of his lips, humming her approval when they parted for her. As if helpless to withstand her sensual assault, he began kissing her back, a soft, moist fusing of their mouths that made Elena go weak with desire. She couldn't recall the last time she'd felt this hot, sweet yearning for a man.

His arms came slowly around her, holding her captive as he plundered her mouth, his tongue sliding against hers with expert precision. Elena welcomed his heat and strength, and she could feel her body blossom beneath his touch, as if anticipating their joining.

She was unprepared when Chase dragged his mouth from hers. "We can't do this," he muttered, trailing his lips over her cheek until he found the soft juncture of her throat and pressed his lips to her hammering pulse.

"We can't *not* do this," she whispered back. "Please... I really need this."

She needed to feel connected to someone, to be touched and held and reminded that she was a desirable woman. It had been so long since she'd felt wanted by a man. Maybe that was partly her own fault for holding herself so rigidly in check, but the prospect of spending the next six months alone was almost too daunting to contemplate. Just for tonight, she wanted this physical bond. She needed it. She needed this man, with his amazing physique and heart-stopping smile, to want her as much as she wanted him.

His breathing was uneven in her ear. "We might never see each other again."

Elena arched her neck, granting him better access. "I understand that, I really do. But you'd be doing me a huge favor if you stayed with me tonight. Please..." She threaded her fingers through his short hair, enjoying the velvet texture and feeling the warmth of his scalp beneath her fingertips. "Stay."

She was glad he didn't ask if she was sure.

She wasn't.

She'd never done anything this reckless or bold in her life, but there was no way she was going to stop. She wanted to experience this man and everything he had to offer, even if it couldn't last for more than one night. She would never say so to Chase, but there was a part of her that was grateful she wouldn't see him again after tonight. If she didn't see him again, he could never disappoint her.

"Please," she repeated.

He didn't argue. He simply swept her into his arms before she could utter another word and carried her into the room, kicking the door closed behind them. Elena had never before had a man pick her up so effortlessly, and there was a part of her that thrilled in his strength and the way it made her feel.

Feminine.

Fragile.

He set her on her feet next to the bed and without giving her a chance to move an inch, cupped her face in his hands and slanted his mouth across hers.

"I could kiss you like this all night," he murmured. "You have the softest lips..."

Tilting her head back, he worked his way down her throat, planting soft kisses and gentle bites against her flesh, until Elena shivered with need. His fingers unhurriedly worked the buttons of her red blouse, until she felt cool air waft against her bare skin. She didn't object when he pushed the shirt from her shoulders and drew her sleeves down, letting the garment drop to the floor until she stood before him in just her bra and jeans.

"Let me look at you," he said, his voice husky. Stepping back, he leaned over and flicked on the bedside lamp.

Elena blinked against the sudden intrusion of light in the dark room, and then blushed as she realized Chase was staring at her. Only he wasn't just looking at her, he was devouring her with his gaze, and the expression in his eyes made Elena feel both excited and nervous.

"What's this?" he asked, and reaching out, he touched the necklace that nestled between her breasts, his fingertips brushing against her sensitized skin and sending jolts of awareness shooting through her.

"Something my sisters gave to me," she said breathlessly, showing him the tiny silver angel charm that dangled from the chain. "It's a guardian angel, to watch over me."

"He'd better do his job," he said huskily, letting the little charm drop back between her breasts. "Lucky little angel."

"I've, um, never done anything like this before," she admitted. Her bones felt deliciously weak, and although she suspected part of it was a result of the absinthe, the major cause was the man who stood looking at her with pure, male appreciation.

"You don't have to do anything now," he assured her. "We could just—" He broke abruptly off with a laugh. "Hell, I don't know…we could just *cuddle*. You don't have to do anything you don't want to."

"But that's just it," she said. "I *want* to do this."

Elena realized it was the truth. And not just because she was leaving in the morning for some remote base whose name she couldn't even pronounce. She wanted this beautiful man and the promise of pleasure that lurked in his eyes. She'd never felt this kind of gnawing lust before. Ever. Her gaze dropped to his lush mouth and a sharp stab of desire speared through her. His lips were too tempting.

Keeping her eyes locked with his, Elena reached behind her and unfastened the clasp of her bra. She didn't miss how Chase swallowed hard. Elena didn't immediately let the undergarment go, but held it pressed against her breasts.

"When I first saw you back there at the party, I wondered…" Her voice trailed off as his gaze sharpened on her.

"What?" His voice sounded hoarse. "What did you wonder?"

"...what you would taste like in my mouth."

"Oh, Christ," he groaned, and in the next instant Elena was in his arms.

She half expected him to pick her up and toss her onto the bed. Instead, he stroked his hands over her bare skin, his fingers finding the dips and curves of her body with infinite care. His turned his face into the arch of her neck and pressed his mouth against her throat. Then he tugged the bra free from her fingers and let it fall to the floor.

Elena didn't have time to feel self-conscious before he covered one breast with his big hand, gently massaging her pliant flesh. She could feel the hard calluses on his palms and gasped at the sensations his touch created, unfamiliar with the cravings rising in her body.

She tipped her head back enough to see his face, and realized his eyes were a mix of browns and greens with flecks of pure gold, surrounded by thick lashes. With his eyes, cheekbones and delectable mouth, the only thing that kept him from too being perfect was his nose, which showed evidence of having been broken at some point.

As he cupped her breast, Elena pushed her hands beneath the hem of his T-shirt. He reflexively tensed, and her fingers skimmed over ridges of muscle across his abdomen. Larry had been a runner, and while he'd been lean, his body had lacked true definition. But not this man; he was sculpted in ways that Elena had never experienced before. She slid her hands higher, reveling in his warm, hard flesh.

He watched her the entire time, and the only indication that her touch affected him was the way his breathing hitched when her fingertips stroked over the small nubs of his nipples.

"Take this off," she said softly, and he complied instantly, reaching behind his head to grab a fistful of shirt and drag it upward.

Elena couldn't prevent a small indrawn breath.

Her first impression had been right; his was a body designed for a woman's touch, and she was helpless to stop herself from running her hand over his chest. She took note of the small scars and imperfections, realizing she knew nothing of him or what he had experienced.

"I was right," she murmured, tracing a long, thin scar that slashed over his ribs. "You're tough."

To her surprise, he laughed. "Oh, yeah. I'm real tough. That's why I have absolutely no willpower where you're concerned."

Elena slid her arms around his waist until they were skin to skin, absorbing the feel of him. "I'm glad. I don't want you to have any willpower tonight."

With a rough sound, Chase lowered his head and caught her mouth in a kiss so deep that she felt it all the way to her toes. She didn't object when he backed her up to the bed and pushed her gently down across the coverlet, following alongside her.

The bedspread was cool against her bare back, but Chase's skin was hot against her breasts. Dragging his mouth from hers, he worked his way unhurriedly down her throat and over her chest, nuzzling her breasts with his mouth. Elena watched him, spellbound by the sight of his dark head against her pale skin, and feeling the rush of heat and wetness between her legs. When he took a nipple into his mouth and drew deeply on the stiffened tip, she gasped and arched upward, clutching at his shoulders.

He tormented first one breast and then the other,

ignoring how Elena twisted beneath him, her hips shifting restlessly against his. He used his mouth to worship her body, moving from her breasts to her stomach, where he teased her navel with his tongue. His fingers moved to the waistband of her jeans and released the fastening in one easy flick of his fingers.

"Yes," she panted, as he slowly drew the zipper down. She lifted her hips, and Chase dragged the jeans down the length of her legs until she lay on the bed wearing nothing but her panties.

"Oh, man," he breathed, "you are so damned pretty."

If Elena had worried that she might not meet his expectations, those doubts vanished beneath the heat in his gaze. Reaching out, she caught him by the waistband of his jeans and tugged until he came over her on all fours, with her fingers still tucked into his pants.

"Take these off," she urged, needing to see him. "Hurry."

Dawn would be here before they knew it, and Elena felt a sudden urgency to meld with this man, to own him and belong to him before it was too late. Even now, her duffel bags lay on the floor by the far wall, packed and ready to go. She suspected that if she were to visit Chase's room, she would see the same.

"I'll take them off," Chase breathed, "but I want to go slow, okay?"

"Okay," she agreed, too eager to see him to tell him that she had no intention of going slow. She was past ready for him. Even now, her panties were soaked with desire, and her sex throbbed with need. She'd listened to her sisters describe lust often enough, but she'd never understood the meaning of the word until now.

Leaning back, Chase unfastened the snap on his jeans, and Elena helped to push them down over his hips. Her breath caught as she saw his erection tenting the material of his cotton boxer shorts. As he stood and kicked his legs free, Elena sat up on the edge of the bed. Reaching out, she laid her hand over the hot ridge of flesh beneath the cotton, thrilling at how he jumped beneath her touch.

"I want to see you," she said, and slid her fingers beneath the stretchy waistband to take him in her hand. His breath hissed in through clenched teeth as she curled her fingers around him, and her body pulsed hotly in response.

"You're gorgeous," she breathed, pushing his boxers down to stroke his length. Glancing upward, she saw Chase watching her through half-closed eyes, his face taut. "You know what I want to do."

"Yeah." His voice came out on a raspy groan.

Elena smiled. She'd never felt so sexy or powerful before in her life. This guy was the embodiment of masculine strength and beauty, and yet she literally held him trembling in the palm of her hand. The effect was an aphrodisiac.

She cupped his weight from beneath with one hand as she trailed her fingers along the velvety shaft with her other. The head of his penis was like a ripe plum, and Elena's mouth watered with the need to taste him. Leaning forward, she ran her tongue lightly over the blunt tip.

"Mmm," she murmured. "You taste delicious." Then she took him fully into her mouth.

Chase made a rough sound, a mixture of surprise and arousal. His hands came up to frame her face, his fingers massaging the tender skin behind her ears. Emboldened, Elena took him deeper, swirling her tongue around him as she used her hand to stroke and caress his length. She pressed her thighs together, squeezing against the sharp throb of arousal between them.

"That's enough," he gasped and eased her away, his breath coming fast. "I won't last if you keep that up, and I'm not ready for this to be over."

Reluctantly, Elena released him and let him push her back onto the mattress. Bending over her, he pressed his mouth against her abdomen. The faint stubble on his jaw abraded the tender skin in a way that made her squirm in delicious anticipation.

"You smell great," he murmured, and hooked his thumbs into the elastic waistband of her panties, pulling them down in one smooth movement. His lips drifted over the arch of her ribs and over the swell of her breasts until he reached a nipple and drew it into his mouth. Elena struggled for breath against the erotic sensations of his tongue and teeth, and she threaded her fingers through his hair, urging him closer.

His warm hand skated over her stomach and lower, urging her legs apart so that he could cup her intimately. Elena's thighs fell open and she pressed upward against his palm, wanting more of the delicious contact.

"That's it," he rasped against her breast, and swirled a finger over her slick flesh, parting her folds and finding the small rise of flesh that thrummed with need. "Oh, man, you're so wet."

He circled a finger over her clitoris, but it wasn't enough. Elena's skin went hot and her sex clenched hungrily. Someone moaned and she realized with a sense of shock that it was her. She needed more. Now.

"Soon," Chase promised, as if reading her mind, and knelt between her splayed knees. He stroked a hand along her inner thigh, urging her legs wider, before he bent down and covered her with his mouth.

Elena gasped and her hips came off the mattress, but Chase held her firmly in place as he laved her with his tongue and lips, alternately sucking and licking until she writhed helplessly. When he began tormenting the tiny bud of her clit, she pushed weakly at his shoulders.

"Please," she finally managed in a strangled voice. "Stop. I can't take any more."

Chase laughed softly, but reached down and grabbed his pants from the floor, fishing through the pockets until he produced a small foil packet. He covered himself quickly, but Elena noticed that his hands seemed unsteady.

He came over her again, bracing himself with his hands on either side of her. "You're sure about this?" he asked. His voice was level, but his breathing was shallow. He wanted her. "If you want me to stop, you have to tell me now, because once I'm inside you, I don't think I can—"

"I'm sure," Elena breathed, and slid her hands along his back to cup his lean buttocks and urge him closer. She felt him nudging against her most private spot, and she opened her legs wider, arching upward to meet him.

"I'm sorry," he grunted. "I can't go slowly—"

He surged forward in one powerful movement, stretching and filling her until he was fully seated inside her. He didn't move for a long moment, his head bent to hers, his breathing ragged.

Elena squeezed experimentally, the walls of her

channel tightening around his flesh. Pleasure lashed through her.

Then he began to move, withdrawing slowly and then sinking back into her in a series of bone-melting strokes. His heated flesh dragged at hers, creating a delicious friction that made Elena arch upward to meet him. The muscles in his arms flexed as he dipped his head and covered her mouth with his, feasting slowly and sensuously on her lips. Elena heard herself whimper softly, and she drew her knees back and hooked her feet around his waist, meeting his thrusts eagerly.

She wanted more.

Chase complied, sliding one arm beneath her to press her more intimately against the hard drive of his body. Elena shivered and clutched at his back.

"Oh, God," she gasped. "You feel so good."

Which was a huge understatement. Had she really told her sister that sex was overrated? If this was what other women experienced with their partners, it was a wonder any of them ever left their beds.

"Damn straight," Chase said, his voice low and rough.

Elena could feel the start of an orgasm building and pushed at his chest.

"Wait," she panted.

Chase raised himself up just enough to look into her face, his own expression taut. "Really? You really want to stop?"

"No. Yes." Elena struggled to think coherently. "I'm getting close, and I don't want this to end yet. I want to try something else."

Chase gave a disbelieving laugh, but his movements slowed and he began to pull back. Elena gritted her teeth and her body followed his, reluctant to release him. She was so close, and she sensed that he was, too. If they continued, he could take her to heaven in a matter of seconds. But suddenly, she wanted to be the one to take him there, to do things that would make him lose control.

She pushed at his shoulders and with a bemused smile he rolled away from her. But Elena didn't give him a chance to question her, covering him swiftly with her own body.

"What? Hey—" He laughed uncertainly, but when Elena dipped her head and traced the whorl of his ear with her tongue, he groaned and collapsed back against the pillows. She pushed his hands up above his head, and slid her own hands down the sensitive undersides of his arms, admiring the impressive bulge of his muscles. Her fingers continued downward, and she scooted backward until she straddled his thighs.

Sitting up, she looked down at him. Her breath caught at the sight he made. He was the embodiment of every fantasy she'd ever had. He lay prone beneath her, but there was nothing remotely relaxed about him. His entire body was rigid and his eyes glittered as he watched her through half-closed lids.

"Now it's my turn," she whispered. "I've always wanted to do this."

She leaned forward until her breasts brushed against his chest, and her angel charm necklace pooled in the depression between his pecs. She traced her lips across his. He cupped the back of her head and drew her down for a more thorough, satisfying kiss. Elena had intended to tease him, to maintain control of their love play until he begged her to release him. But when he smoothed his free hand along her flank and then reached between them to touch her intimately, she knew she was lost.

She gasped into his mouth, and settled more fully against him. He used his hands to splay her thighs even wider where she straddled him. Then there he was, hot and thick, moving into her bit by little bit, until Elena made an incoherent sound of need and pushed back, thrusting him fully into her.

"Ah," he groaned. "That almost feels too good."

Elena silently agreed, and slowly raised herself up until he was nearly free of her body, before pushing herself down once more, burying him to the hilt. The hot, throbbing sensation increased as she moved on top of him, gripping him tightly. His fingers were on her hips, guiding her, and he watched her face through pleasure-glazed eyes. When he slid his hands upward to cup and knead her breasts, Elena closed her eyes in mindless bliss.

"Yes," she breathed. "Oh, yes."

"Look at me."

The words were soft but insistent. She opened her eyes and stared down at Chase, seeing the raw, masculine need and pleasure on his face.

"I want you to look at me when you come," he rasped. His expression had tightened, and the tautness of his body told her he was close to losing control. Seeing his desire mount only served to fuel her own. and his words were enough to send her over the brink. Her orgasm slammed into her, and the only thing anchoring her to Earth were Chase's hands, holding her. She might have closed her eyes but for his soft command.

"Look at me."

As he reached his own climax, their gazes were locked

on one another, until with a last shudder of pleasure, he smiled into her eyes and tugged her down until she lay replete against his chest.

He pressed his lips against her hair, and his hands stroked soothingly down her body. When she turned her face up to his, he kissed her sweetly, and even in the faint light, she could see the softness of his expression. He tucked her closer against his side, and one hand traced lazy patterns on her shoulder and arm. "Hey, you okay?"

A reluctant smile tugged at her lips. "More than okay. I'm great."

"No regrets, then?"

Elena raised herself on her elbow to look at him. He lay against the pillows like a big, sleek cat. "Absolutely no regrets. You've actually fulfilled a lifelong fantasy of mine."

Chase chuckled. "Do you have any other fantasies you'd like to fulfill? Like I said, I'm here to serve."

"As a matter of fact," she murmured, tracing his lower lip with her thumb, "there are a few I'd like to explore."

Chase's eyes sharpened on her with interest. "Oh, yeah? Tell me."

Elena bit her lip, and then leaned forward and whispered softly in his ear. When she drew back, she looked at him with apprehension in her eyes.

"Oh, man," Chase said with a soft groan, pulling her down so that she lay sprawled across him, her breasts flattened against his chest. "We have about five hours before dawn. I may just die trying to do all those things, but I promise you I'm going to go out a happy man."

4

MAJOR DUMFRIES had been right about one thing—
flying in a helicopter while nursing a hangover was no
fun. At least, not after the first ten minutes, when the
initial thrill had faded and Elena found herself painfully
conscious of the cold. Before long, her bottom started to
ache from the weight of the armored vest that she was
required to wear. The constant whir of the rotor blades
was deafening, until she was no longer sure if they were
coming from the helicopter or inside her head.

Elena wasn't even sure if the total exhaustion she felt
was a result of the absinthe she'd consumed, or a combination of too little sleep and too much unaccustomed
physical activity. Her body felt deliciously tender from
her night with Chase, and each small movement brought
back memories.

She couldn't stop thinking about him, or about what
they'd done together. Last night had been an anomaly.
She'd acted completely out of character, but then again,
she'd never met a man like Chase McCormick before.
With Larry, she'd always tamped down her own desires
and contented herself with their standard missionary-

style sex. At least, she'd thought she was content with the routine coitus, but now she knew differently. She'd been going through the motions, and while she'd had some pleasant orgasms with Larry, none of it could compare to what she'd experienced with Chase.

The man was a master, and Elena had come alive under his expert touch. She hadn't known she was capable of such uninhibited passion. After that first amazing hour, they'd slept briefly. Elena had woken to find Chase propped with his head on his hand, watching her. The heat in his expression had made it impossible for Elena to feel embarrassed. Instead, an answering warmth had bloomed low in her abdomen. Without a word, he'd circled his thumb over her nipple and they'd both watched the small bud tighten beneath his touch. Finally, unable to stand it any longer, she had rubbed herself against him, sliding her leg over his hips and letting him know she was more than ready for him again.

Afterward, Chase had pulled her into his arms and she'd again drifted into sleep to the sound of his heartbeat thumping steadily beneath her ear. But when her alarm clock had finally gone off, she had found herself alone. While she'd told herself it was for the best, she couldn't deny feeling bereft at Chase's absence. He'd told her he'd have to leave before dawn, but even knowing that he had his own flight to catch hadn't been enough to keep her from feeling abandoned. She'd wanted to savor every bit of their short time together. If she closed her eyes, she could still feel Chase's warm body and his lips against her temple. Being with him was the closest to heaven that she would ever get.

And now she'd never see him again.

Elena looked around at the other occupants of the

helicopter. They were a group of fifteen civilians, with just one other woman besides herself. The woman was quite a bit older than Elena, in her early fifties at least. Dressed in the DPA uniform of black cargo pants and fleece jacket, she seemed frail and nervous. Her gray hair stuck out at odd angles beneath her baseball cap, and she continually smoothed it with her fingers, tucking the strands back in. Elena felt a rush of sympathy for the woman, wondering what had prompted her to volunteer for this deployment and if she had also been destined for a different location.

When Elena had arrived at the military airstrip, she'd been surprised to learn they wouldn't be flying on one of the military helicopters, but on a commercially chartered one. But they'd had to wait awhile before the helicopter had been ready to depart, giving Elena plenty of time to think about the previous night.

She'd had a one-night stand with a complete stranger.

She'd thought she'd feel cheapened and used. Guilty. But she felt none of those things. Instead, she found herself smiling each time she recalled the previous night. Chase had made her feel incredibly sexy, and she couldn't bring herself to regret the pleasure she'd shared with him. He'd been so attuned to her, anticipating the needs of her body before she did. He'd been tender and masterful, and they'd fitted together as if they'd been made for each other.

Casual conversation was almost impossible on board the helicopter, given the noise of the engine and the rotors, so Elena contented herself with looking out the window at the changing view. They flew high for several hours, the land beneath them turning harsh and rugged.

As they began to descend, Elena could just make out a compound in the distance. The base looked small and vulnerable in the vast openness that surrounded it, and only the distant mountains gave any relief to the stark landscape.

As the helicopter drew closer, Elena couldn't help but stare openmouthed as the base came fully into view. Even by military standards it was heavily fortified, surrounded by walls of sandbags and razor-wire fencing. She could see row after row of small huts, and then an area of hangars. More than half of the base was occupied by military vehicles of all sizes.

They landed on a helicopter pad on the far side of the base, and when the doors finally swung open, Elena was greeted by a blast of hot, dry air. A soldier, dressed in full battle gear and helmet poked his head into the passenger compartment where Elena sat with the others. His mouth creased into a smile, revealing white teeth in his tanned face.

"Welcome to Forward Operating Base Sharlana!" He had to shout to be heard over the engines as they wound down. "I'm Staff Sergeant Mike Corrente. I hope you had a pleasant flight. If you'll disembark and grab your gear, I'll show you to your quarters."

He spoke rapidly, and with such a strong Boston accent that Elena had a difficult time understanding him. She struggled into her backpack and climbed down, clapping a hand over her head to keep her hat from flying off from the downward wash of the rotors. She refused the sergeant's proffered hand, but she didn't miss how his blue eyes sharpened on her with interest as she stepped past him. She waited with the others while he and a second soldier began unceremoniously tossing their duffel bags out of the helicopter and onto the dusty ground.

Elena took the opportunity to survey their surroundings. Everything—from the helicopter and the nearby fleet of military vehicles, to the surrounding plains and distant mountains—was a uniform shade of dull brown.

After several moments of searching for her bags, Elena grunted with effort as she slung her first duffel over her shoulder and then hefted her second with her free hand.

"Okay, folks, listen up," Corrente called. He spoke with authority and Elena found herself wondering what position he held on the base. "I'll show you where you'll be staying, and you'll each have a couple of hours to rest before dinner. After that, we'll head over the rec center for orientation and a quick tour of the facility. The sooner you understand the battle rhythm here at Sharlana, the quicker you'll be able to adapt to life on a forward operating base, but don't expect any preferential treatment. Everyone on this base is responsible for their own quality of life. So grab your gear and follow me."

"How far is it to our quarters?" asked the older woman, looking across the expanse of tarmac to the hangars and tiny, plywood huts. There wasn't a single building in sight that resembled a dormitory or other living quarters.

"Not far," the sergeant said cheerfully. "See those buildings over there? Your quarters are just on the other side."

Elena saw the other woman's face blanch and felt sympathy for her. Her own head was pounding and the helicopter trip had left her feeling slightly queasy. That, combined with the oppressive heat, made even the slightest physical exertion a supreme effort. Under different conditions, she would have offered to carry the other woman's baggage for her, but it was all she could do to manage her own.

"I can carry that duffel bag for you, ma'am," Corrente said to the older woman, correctly interpreting her expression of dismay.

"Well, I don't know," the woman demurred. "If you're sure..."

"Absolutely, ma'am," he said with a grin. "It keeps me in shape."

She relinquished her bag to the younger man with a grateful smile. "Thank you so much. Maybe it's the flight, but I'm feeling a little peaked."

"Probably the altitude," the sergeant replied. "You'll get used to it."

Elena doubted it. She walked behind the two soldiers and the other civilians, hoping she didn't embarrass herself by passing out. She hadn't eaten anything all day, and she was starting to feel a little shaky. Sweat popped out along her brow and her shirt clung damply to her skin. The helicopter churned up clouds of dust, and her mouth felt thick and dry.

"Ma'am, can I take those bags for you?"

Elena looked around in surprise to see the second soldier speaking to her. He had reddish hair and a good-natured expression, and Elena found herself smiling back at him. He indicated her duffel bags. "Those look heavy."

"Oh, no," she said quickly, recalling the sergeant's remark about not receiving preferential treatment. "I can manage."

His quick grin and raised eyebrows clearly said, "Yeah, right." But instead of voicing his skepticism, he reached out firmly and took one duffel bag from her.

"I insist," he said. "I'll catch hell from my C.O. if I let you pass out before you've even checked in. Besides, it's easier to carry your gear than to have to carry you *and* your gear if you collapse."

Elena knew enough military jargon to know that C.O. stood for Commanding Officer, so she gave him another smile and let him take her other bag.

"Thank you so much," she said, falling into step beside him. "It must be the heat that makes me feel so tired. I'm Elena de la Vega, by the way."

"I'm Corporal Cleary, but you can call me Pete. Where're you from?"

"Virginia. I work for the Defense Procurement Agency."

He nodded. "We have a bunch of DPA folks on the base. What kind of work will you be doing?"

"I'll be working at the contracting center. I'll be overseeing the construction projects you have on base, as well as working with the contractors to ensure everything gets done on time." A breeze wafted across her face, bringing with it a putrid stench that made Elena recoil and clap a hand over her nose and mouth. "Oh, my god," she gasped. "What is that smell?"

Pete grinned. "I'd say that's your first project. We've been trying to install a waste water treatment facility on the base, but without too much success. We're having trouble getting the parts needed for the plant. What you're smelling is the cesspool at the back of the base. Nice, huh?"

Elena looked at him in disbelief and horror. "You're kidding, right?"

"Nope," he said cheerfully. "You get used to the smell. Well, mostly you get used to it. Sometimes it's so bad that it wakes me up from a sound sleep. We're almost there."

They passed a group of four men wearing ragged clothing and traditional Middle Eastern headgear. They sported beards and shaggy hair and as they drew alongside Elena and her companions, they deliberately averted their gazes.

"Who are they?" she asked, keeping her voice low. Because really, they looked a lot like the pictures of terrorists she'd seen so many times on the six o'clock news. And while she'd known she would have contact with the local people on some level, she hadn't been prepared for her own reaction of mistrust.

"Those are some of the locals. We have a dozen or so who come to work on the base each day. Task force Peacemaker also runs construction workshops for local men. Each man learns basic wood, concrete and masonry construction techniques, and at the end of the workshop we provide them with tools that they can bring back to their villages. The men we just passed are all graduates of the workshops."

Elena glanced over her shoulder at the retreating men. "How do you know if they're…you know…"

"Trustworthy? We do a background check on everyone who comes onto the base. Those are the good guys. But they're still funny about interacting with women, so don't take it personally if they steer clear of you."

So he had noticed how the men had studiously avoided acknowledging either Elena or the other woman.

"Trust me," she assured him. "No offense taken. I'd be freaked out if any of them looked twice at me. Should I cover my hair or something?"

She was half joking, but Pete didn't laugh. He looked deadly serious. "Not here on the base, but if you go outside the fence I'd recommend you wear a head covering under your helmet. Just to keep from offending anyone."

Elena digested this information, wondering how often she would be required to leave the base. She'd be just as happy if she never ventured beyond the fence.

They were walking between rows of the huts that she had glimpsed from the helicopter. There were dozens of them, side by side. Constructed of simple plywood, each had a door and two tiny windows, and were identical in appearance.

"What are these used for?" she asked. "Storage?"

Pete glanced at her with a quizzical smile. "Kinda. They're called *chews*."

Elena laughed. "Okay, I give up. Why are they called chews?"

"It's an acronym for containerized housing unit. You know…CHU…*chew*. One of these will be your home while you're at Sharlana. We bunk eight to a CHU. Under ideal conditions, civilians get to bunk with other civilians, but we just had a special ops team and two light-infantry units arrive this morning, so we're tight on housing. You'll have one other civilian and six military females in your CHU."

Elena stared at him in disbelief. "I thought I'd have my own housing unit."

Pete laughed. "Sorry, but that's a luxury we can't afford around here. Maybe that's the case in Baghdad, but out here only the big guns get their own units. We're building more, but it's doubtful that civilians will ever have their own private quarters, and the showers will always be open bay. But it's a hell of a sight better than the tents we used to live in."

They were walking past an area that was cordoned off from the rest of the base. A wire fence had been draped with camouflage netting, effectively preventing anyone from seeing what lay on the other side. As they walked past, Elena thought she could glimpse buildings and movement through the netting. She eyed the signs that hung from the fence that read No Admittance.

"What's this area used for?" she asked. "Detainees?"

Pete followed her gaze. "This is where the special ops guys hang out. Due to the sensitive nature of their jobs, they mostly work here or over at the Tactical Operations Center. Sometimes you'll see them at the dining facility." He shrugged. "Not that you'd be able to tell them apart from the rest of us, unless they grow their beards out."

"Oh." Elena peered through the netting as they passed, curious in spite of herself. She'd heard about the special ops guys, of course. Who hadn't? They were the unseen heroes of the war on terror, going where angels feared to tread, and getting out again without anyone realizing they had even been there. She pictured them as bearded and hard-eyed, dressed in clothing that would permit them to blend in with the local population.

From behind the fence, she could hear masculine whoops and shouts, and then a surprising cheer went up.

"Doesn't sound like secret work to me," she commented.

Pete shrugged. "A new team of guys just arrived this morning, and the team that's been here for the past year is getting ready to head home. They'll spend a couple of days transitioning. But right now they have ten guys behind that fence, which is enough for a serious game of touch football." He glanced at Elena. "It's important to let off steam, especially with these guys."

Up ahead, a gate in the fence swung open, and a figure emerged. Even from a distance, Elena could see he was dressed casually in a pair of shorts and a T-shirt, with a baseball cap pulled low over his eyes. With his tanned legs and sandals, he could have been a tourist. Only the assault rifle slung across his back indicated he wasn't what he appeared. He glanced at the group before turning away, and then stopped and slowly swung back in their direction.

Elena heard Pete mutter a curse under his breath.

"What's wrong?" she asked.

"I'm not sure," he replied. "But when a special ops guy decides you're worth a second look, it can't be good."

Elena followed Pete's gaze and saw the man striding purposefully toward them. This guy was special ops? He was silhouetted against the setting sun, and Elena had to shield her eyes to see him. Despite his casual clothing, everything about him said he meant business. But what could he possibly want with a group of civilians?

"I told you I could carry my own gear," she said to Pete, apprehension tickling her spine. "Are you in trouble?"

"Nah. Like I said, it was that or carry you *and* your gear." He shrugged, clearly puzzled. "I have no idea what this guy wants. But it's obvious that he thinks he outranks us, which means he probably does. Which means we'll respectfully listen to whatever it is he has to say."

"Soldiers, front and center!"

Elena craned for a better view of the man who spoke in such authoritative tones, but the group in front of her blocked her. Still, there was something very familiar about that voice.

Pete dropped her duffel bags and made his way toward the front. Elena edged forward, too. She watched as both soldiers came rigidly to attention before the man in the shorts, who stood, arms akimbo, surveying them through grim eyes.

Elena barely suppressed a gasp and her heart exploded into action. There was no way...it couldn't be! But as she swiped the sweat and grit from her eyes and peered again, there was no doubt in her mind. The man was none other than the one she thought she'd never see again...Chase McCormick.

Adrenaline, hot and dizzying, buzzed through her veins. Her blood pounded in her ears, and her first instinct was to turn tail and run. To hide. Because there was no way she could face him, not after last night. Not when he hadn't even said goodbye, but had slipped out of her room while she'd slept.

What was he doing here? She'd been so certain she would never run into him again, and although she'd liked him—really, really liked him—she would have preferred it that way. She wasn't sophisticated enough to act as if nothing had happened. Already every cell in her body was reacting to seeing him. But last night he'd been a different man, warm and solid and safe whereas right now he seemed every inch a warrior. Beneath the ball cap, his eyes were hidden behind a pair of dark sunglasses, but Elena could feel the weight of his scrutiny and knew with certainty that *she* was the reason he'd turned around and intercepted them.

She blushed and stepped casually behind one of the other civilians, out of his range of vision, hoping that she was wrong, and that he didn't recognize her beneath the DPA cap she wore. Just seeing him again caused her body to thrum with recalled pleasure. What were the chances that he would be here, at the same forward operating base as her? It was almost enough to make her believe in fate.

In the next instant, she wondered how he would react when he realized she would be working in proximity with him for the next six months. Would he be horrified to see his one-night stand turn up on his doorstep? Or would he think their prior encounter gave him rights for future hookups? The sex had been off the charts, but no way did she want to become his go-to girl every time he had an itch that needed scratching. She wouldn't be used. Not by him. Not by anyone.

He was speaking to the two soldiers in low tones while they stood rigidly at attention. When he was through, they both gave a loud "Yessir!" and turned back to the group.

"If you'll follow me," Pete said to the group, "I'll show each of you to your designated quarters. You'll have several hours to unpack and rest, and then I'll return to escort you to the chow hall."

Elena didn't miss how he gave her a cheeky wink, but as she bent to retrieve her two duffel bags, a shadow fell over her.

"Not you, Miss de la Vega," said a cool voice.

Elena glanced up to see Chase standing beside her.

This was definitely not the same, user-friendly version she'd known in Kuwait. He didn't fool her with his casual, tourist clothing and day's growth of beard. With his set jaw and a seriously badass weapon slung across his back, he still looked like a tough, hardened soldier. He'd removed his sunglasses and Elena felt her insides quiver at the expression in his eyes.

"I'll see you in private," he said quietly. "Now."

Without waiting to see if she would follow him, he turned on his heel and began striding away, while the other civilians gaped at her. Under any other circumstances, Elena would have looked forward to the prospect of getting some private time with Chase. But the rigid set of his shoulders as he walked away told her that this encounter wouldn't be of a romantic nature.

"Who is that man? And how does he know who you are?" the other woman asked Elena. "Is he your new boss?"

Elena struggled beneath the burden of her two duffel bags. "We met last night in Kuwait," she explained hurriedly. "But I don't really know him. And he is definitely not my boss."

She averted her gaze from the knowing looks and followed Chase, feeling like a schoolgirl who'd just been called to the principal's office. She reminded herself that she'd done nothing wrong. She had no reason to feel so apprehensive about what he might say.

Even then, she couldn't help but admire Chase's legs as he strode away. They were muscled and tanned, and she recalled all too well how powerful they were.

He climbed the steps of a small hut that sported a small, curtained window on either side of the door. A sign over the doorway read Tactical Operations Center.

Dropping her gear on the dusty ground outside the building, Elena followed him inside. She found herself in a crudely furnished office, with a desk built out of plywood and two-by-fours, and shelving crafted from stacked wooden crates. Two soldiers sat working at computer stations in the small space, and they looked up as Chase and Elena entered, their faces expressing surprise and interest.

"Can you give us a moment?" Chase asked quietly, his voice brooking no argument.

The men got up, nodding politely to Elena as they passed. The space was crammed with state-of-the-art computer and radio equipment, and an enormous map of Afghanistan covered one wall. On the opposite wall was a row of photos of men dressed in traditional Middle Eastern garb, with their names in bold print below them. Elena realized these were pictures of terrorists that the military hoped to capture or kill. In that instant, the full impact of where she was hit her.

Chase slid the weapon from his shoulder and placed it on a nearby surface. As he looked at her, Elena could see that he wasn't just upset, he was furious. "What the hell are you doing here, Elena?"

"I could ask you the same question."

Chase arched an eyebrow. "This is my fourth deployment to Afghanistan and my second time at this particular base. I'm active-duty military. This is what I do. But you're a civilian, so I'll ask you again. What are you doing here?"

"I work for the DPA. This is where they've sent me."

He cursed and raked one hand through his hair. Elena

watched, mesmerized, recalling the silky texture of those strands.

"You told me you were going to Shangri-la. I thought it was a joke. At the time, I figured you were heading back to the States."

Elena arched an eyebrow at him. "Sorry to disappoint you. I couldn't recall the name of the base, only that it sounded like Shangri-la."

Chase made a gesture of frustration. "I checked the manifest this morning, and it said you were going to Baghdad, to the Green Zone."

He'd checked the manifest! That information wasn't available to just anyone, and Elena was warmed to think he'd cared enough to find out where she was going.

"Obviously you didn't go to Iraq," he continued. "So how the hell did you end up on my base?"

Elena frowned, not liking his tone. Was he implying that she'd purposely come to Sharlana because she knew he was here? "I don't know what manifesto you were looking at, but I can assure you that I am assigned to this base. Originally, yes, I was supposed to go to Iraq, but my orders got changed at the last minute." She hesitated. "Do you have a particular problem with my being here?"

"Damn straight I have a problem with it." He took a step toward her, his gaze raking over her. "This is no place for a woman, and certainly not a woman like you."

Elena bristled. "And just what is that supposed to mean?"

Chase made a growling sound of frustration. "Jesus, Elena, do I need to spell it out? Look at you! You have no military background, no experience with life on a forward operating base. This place is hard enough for men to deal with, without having the added burden of a civilian female to worry about."

Elena's chin lifted. "I can take care of myself, Chase. Besides, there's another civilian woman here. Why aren't you bitching at her, too?"

He frowned. "I am not bitching at you. I'm just telling you that Sharlana is not an easy place to live. Besides," he swept her with another cold glance, "I saw the other woman and I can assure you that she's unlikely to distract the men, whereas you…"

"Oh. My. God." Elena stared at him in dawning comprehension. "I can't believe this." She gave a disbelieving laugh. "You are such a male chauvinist!"

"I am not a male chauvinist," he protested. "I just happen to believe that there are certain places a woman doesn't belong, and here is one of them."

"Why?" she challenged. "Because you think I'll distract the men? That's ludicrous."

"Is it?" he asked drily. "The men on this base have explicit instructions not to give females—or civilians— preferential treatment. Yet there they were, carrying your gear like a couple of lackeys."

"I was tired. Pete was being a gentleman."

"*Pete?*" he repeated in disbelief. "Jesus, you just met the guy ten minutes ago and you're already on a first-name basis?"

"Why not?" Her tone was deceptively silken. "Look where you and I were after just twenty minutes."

His eyes grew hot, and if Elena hadn't known better, she might have thought he was jealous.

"He's not *Pete*," he ground out. "He's Corporal Cleary and he's on duty. This isn't a Virginia tearoom, Miss de la Vega, and there are no bellhops or doormen to do your bidding. Here, everyone pulls their own weight or they get sent home."

"I bet you'd like that, wouldn't you?" Elena asked, feeling equally hurt and angered by his manner. To think, she'd actually been excited to see him again.

"Damn straight I would. In fact, I may just insist upon it."

"You wouldn't!" Elena gasped, outraged. "I came here to do a job, and I'm not leaving just because you're uncomfortable having me around." She hesitated as a thought struck her. "If it's about last night…"

"It's not," he insisted. "I'd feel the same way if I'd never seen you before today. But since you brought it up, now is a good time to inform you that sex is not permitted on this base. Or any other military installation in the Middle Eastern theater, for that matter."

"Don't worry," Elena snapped, giving him what she hoped was a disdainful look. "There's nobody—*nobody*—here that I'm interested in having sex with."

"Good," he snapped back. "You might want to make that clear to *Pete*."

Elena narrowed her eyes. Could it be possible that he *was* jealous? She might have forgiven his obnoxious behavior if she thought that was the cause, but he'd made it clear that he was less than happy to see her. More likely, he was one of those old-school kind of guys who thought a woman's place was in the bedroom.

"I can't believe we're even having this conversation," Elena said. "Pete—Corporal Cleary—said that you're special ops, and I realize they don't let women into their ranks. But in case you haven't noticed, women have finally been accepted in the military."

"Oh, I've noticed," he said meaningfully.

"But you don't like it," Elena finished for him.

Chase made a growling sound and Elena was unprepared when he advanced on her. "You're not getting it. Out here, *this is a man's world*. I don't have a problem with women in the military. I have a problem with assigning women—especially civilian women—to troops that in the past have been designated as all male."

"And why is that?" she asked. She tipped her chin up, but took an involuntary step backward. "Because you think we can't handle it?"

"No," he snarled. "Because I don't think the *men* can handle it. Think about it. There are lots of young males and damn few females here. The men can't go outside the base to look for sex, so they look inside. The shortage of women creates competition and poisons the work atmosphere with distrust and animosity, not to mention lust. Even if the situation doesn't erupt into overt rape, it will always be disruptive and undermine the cohesion, morale and discipline that these missions require. Now do you get it?"

Elena's heart hammered hard in her chest. "Are you saying I'm in danger from your men?" she finally asked, swallowing hard.

"I'm saying that you need to think long and hard before you bat your eyelashes in their direction, or play the damsel in distress and have one of them come running to carry your gear." He swept her with a long look. "Nobody could blame them for getting the wrong idea. Some of these boys have been out here for a year or more, and any one of them would bend over backward for just a smile from you."

"But not you."

Even as the words left her mouth, Elena wished them back. She sounded bitter and jealous, and the last thing she wanted was for Chase to think that she wanted *him* to notice her in that way, or to bend over backward to please *her.*

"No," he agreed quietly. "Not me. There's a time and place for that, and it's not here. And while we're at it, you're to address me as First Sergeant McCormick or sir, is that clear?"

"Perfectly," Elena retorted, her voice as chilly as his.

"Try to understand. We're in a combat environment, Elena, and each person on this base has a responsibility to see to their own safety. You'll receive no special treatment from me or any of the other men," he continued, "so if you can't handle that, you should think about leaving."

"Not a chance," she snapped. "I'm here to stay, *sir,* and the sooner you get that through your head, the easier it will be for *you.* Are we done here?"

"We're done. Just remember what I've said, Elena. The rules are for your own safety."

Elena snorted her disbelief. "Just tell me where my quarters are so that I can go and clean up." She swept him with a scathing look. "And while we're at it, I'll ask you to address me as Ms. de la Vega or *ma'am.*"

She watched as his lips tightened. Had she really thought his mouth delectable? He was a bastard, through and through, and her only regret was that she'd actually enjoyed their night together. More than enjoyed it. Sex with Chase McCormick had eclipsed every other pleasure she'd experienced in her life.

This whole horrible encounter would have been so

much easier if he'd been terrible in bed, but the fact was he'd been amazing. All three times. And as much as she told herself that she was better off having nothing to do with him, a part of her desperately wanted a repeat performance.

5

FROM THE DOORWAY of his office, Chase watched Elena struggle to carry her duffel bags. Her slender shoulders bowed under their weight, and his hands clenched at his sides. Every instinct in his body demanded that he go down and help her. He'd seen the shadows under her eyes. She was exhausted, and he was largely to blame. She hadn't gotten any sleep because of him.

Memories of the previous night rushed back, and he ran a hand across his eyes to dispel the erotic images. He'd known it would be a huge mistake to sleep with Elena, yet he'd been unable to resist. She was too tempting. Too feminine. Too entirely appealing.

But as much as he physically wanted her, he absolutely didn't want her at Sharlana. The remote, mountainous region frequently came under attack from the Taliban, and current intelligence reports suggested another one could come at any time. The recent death of eight civilians at the hands of insurgents less than fifty miles away only served to emphasize the danger they were in.

What if he couldn't keep her safe?

More than six months had passed since he'd witnessed

the ambush on the supply convoy in Iraq, but he'd never forget how the gunner had abandoned his post to try and protect the female truck driver, and they'd both been shot by insurgents as a result. After the attack, Chase had made inquiries and learned that both soldiers would survive their injuries. He'd also learned that the two soldiers had been romantically involved.

The experience had only confirmed his belief that women had no place in combat. Most men of his acquaintance had been raised to believe that women were weaker and required protection. To expect those same men to let a woman fend for herself in combat was unrealistic. Better to keep the woman out of danger in the first place.

Just the thought of anything happening to Elena caused his chest to tighten and a sick sensation to unfurl in his stomach. He didn't object to civilians working alongside the military, but he seriously objected to civilian women—especially Elena—being sent to remote bases like Sharlana. The conditions were too harsh. Even if he could ensure her safety, she wasn't cut out for life on a forward operating base.

She was soft. Literally. Even now, he could recall the satiny texture of her skin, feel the lushness of her lips pressed against his. She wasn't a woman who was accustomed to physical exertion; the demands he'd made on her last night had left her weak as a kitten. He couldn't envision her lasting through an Afghan winter.

She'd been asleep when the alarm on his wristwatch had gone off, reminding him that he had less than forty minutes to change into his combat gear, grab his shit and make it to the airstrip. Not wanting to wake her up, he'd scrawled a brief note on the hotel stationery and had tucked it into her duffel bag for her to find later. He'd had just enough time to stop by the embassy and scan the most recent lists, where he'd been relieved to find her name among those scheduled to go to Camp Victory in Baghdad. Shangri-la, indeed. At the large military base, she'd have all the amenities of home, including fast-food restaurants, shopping opportunities and decent living quarters. Most importantly, she'd be well protected. He just hadn't realized that her orders had been changed since that list had been printed.

When he'd first caught sight of her walking across the base at Sharlana, he'd been stunned. He'd thought of her more than he cared to admit—even to himself—since he'd left her bed. At first he'd believed he was imagining things; that he wanted her so much that his mind was playing tricks on him. His next reaction had been a fierce pleasure at seeing her again, followed immediately by anger. What the hell was she doing here? For a brief instant, he'd wondered if she'd somehow learned where he was headed and had managed to follow him. But according to Elena, she was at Sharlana on legitimate business as a contract administrator, although he intended to find out why her orders had been changed at the last minute. And the hell of it was, he couldn't do a damn thing about it. He was special ops; he and his men only used Sharlana as an operating base for covert forays across the border into Pakistan. He had no authority over Elena, and even his threats to have her sent back to the States didn't carry any weight.

Only she didn't know that.

As he watched her from the doorway, Corporal Cleary approached Elena. He glanced in Chase's direction and almost defiantly reached out and took the duffel bags from Elena. Chase watched as Elena tried to argue with him, but Cleary shook his head and continued walking until Elena had no choice but to follow him.

Chase frowned, unfamiliar with the odd, clenching sensation in his chest. He wanted to be the one walking Elena to her new quarters. He wanted to be the guy who made life easier for her—but he wouldn't be a hypocrite. He firmly believed that women had no place on a remote base like Sharlana. Their very presence created a distraction that could prove dangerous, both to themselves and the men who sought to protect them. He wasn't unfeeling, and he'd do what he could to keep them safe, but he couldn't afford to let his men lose their focus.

Elena and Corporal Cleary stopped in front of a hut at the far end of the housing area, about five doors from the unit where Chase himself was staying with his team. He groaned inwardly. Bad enough that they were on the same base, but knowing she was so close would be a distraction that *he* didn't need. Chase blew out a hard breath. He had no clue how he'd stay focused, knowing Elena was just feet away.

ELENA OPENED THE DOOR of her living quarters and stared in dismay at the cramped interior. The space had been divided into eight tiny compartments, each one with a cot and a crudely constructed nightstand and shelf. Elena had expected austere living conditions, but she hadn't been prepared for this. She'd thought Larry was exaggerating when he'd said she'd be sharing a B-hut with twenty other women. Just imagining his smug expression if he knew the truth was enough for her to square her shoulders and step determinedly inside. Sharing space with seven other women would be a piece of cake. She might prefer privacy, but she didn't need it to survive. After all, she'd grown up with two sisters and a mother who had invented the word *drama*. This would be easy by comparison.

The farthest compartment was occupied by the older woman who had traveled with her on the helicopter, and Elena saw she was unpacking her duffel bags and attempting to make her little space homier. Only the tiny cubicle nearest the door was free of personal gear.

"Sergeant Corrente said we could take whichever compartments we wanted, and I didn't want to be near the door," the woman said in way of explanation. "I'm Sylvia Dobbs, by the way. I'm a quality inspector from the San Antonio DPA office. How about you?"

Elena dumped her duffel bags on the floor of the empty cubicle. "I'm Elena de la Vega, from the HQ office. I'll be working at the contracting center."

"It must be nice to actually know somebody here, and especially someone so handsome," Sylvia said, smoothing a small, brightly colored throw blanket over her cot, but Elena didn't miss the curiosity in the other woman's voice.

Elena sat down on the bare mattress of the narrow bed, frowning at the unyielding surface. "I don't really know him. At least not well. And I'm not so sure he's all that happy to see me." She didn't want to talk about Chase. "How long did the sergeant say we had before dinner?"

"An hour or so. Enough time to unpack and maybe catch a quick nap." Sylvia yawned hugely. "I'm wiped out, so I'm going to lay down for a little bit. The sergeant said to tell you that there's a supply office in the warehouse at the end of the road. If you need anything you can get it there. Otherwise, he'll come to get us for dinner, and then we have to attend a base-orientation class with the other folks who came in today."

"Did he say how long that might take?"

"Maybe an hour. He said we'll go over safety and security procedures, then we'll take a quick tour of the base and see where we'll be working while we're here."

"Who's sleeping in the other beds?" Elena asked, noting the photos and stickers that the occupants had affixed to the plywood walls.

"Soldiers," Sylvia said. "Female soldiers. With our luck they probably get up at the crack of dawn."

Elena slanted Sylvia an amused look. "I'm sure we're expected to get up at the crack of dawn, too. I was told we'll be working twelve- and fourteen-hour days, seven days a week. There is no sleeping late."

Sylvia stilled, then resumed smoothing the blankets on her bed. When she spoke, her voice was so quiet that Elena almost didn't hear her. "I hope I didn't make a huge mistake in coming here."

"Why did you come here?"

The other woman turned toward Elena, and hesitated before speaking. "I just went through a nasty divorce. Unfortunately, my ex made out better in the settlement than I did." She shrugged. "I needed a change of scenery, and the money was too good to pass up."

Elena felt a pang of sympathy for her. "I'm sure that being here will take some getting used to, but you'll be fine."

She bounced experimentally on the bed, wincing at the unforgiving surface. Standing up, she examined the cot, seeing that she'd only been provided with a box spring, but no mattress. There was no way she could sleep on the bed without a mattress. She tried to see what Sylvia had on her bed, but the other woman had already covered the surface with her sleeping bag and the throw blanket. The other beds were also covered with sleeping bags, so it was difficult to determine if they had mattresses, or not.

"Maybe I'll take a walk over to the supply office and let you get some sleep." She looked doubtfully around the hut. "He didn't say where the bathroom is located, did he?"

Sylvia grimaced. "Unfortunately, they only have open bay showers and latrines. They're located in the last building on the right, so we passed it coming in."

Elena pulled her baseball cap off and smoothed her hair back from her face. "God, I could use a shower. I feel so sticky. Maybe I'll do that now."

"Oh, Corrente said that they have a water shortage, so showers are limited to just five minutes, and only every other day."

"You're kidding."

"Nope, I'm not. He said that one of the projects they're working on is a well. If they can get the well operational, then we'll have plenty of water, but right now it's being rationed."

Elena stood up, clapping her baseball cap back onto her head. "Great. I'm going over to the supply office. Is there anything you need?"

Sylvia shook her head and stretched out on her bed. "Just some sleep."

Elena left the hut and headed in the direction Sylvia had indicated. Even this late in the afternoon, the heat was oppressive, stealing her breath and baking down on her shoulders. Two helicopters flew low over the base, the sound of their engines overpowering. Elena shielded her eyes to watch them pass, then immediately covered her face as eddies of dust swirled through the air, kicked up by the rotor blades. Swearing softly, she brushed the grit from her eyes and continued walking. She passed several groups of soldiers along the narrow street and although they stared at her with undisguised interest, they were polite enough in their greetings, addressing her with a nod and a curt "Ma'am."

With her DPA uniform of black cargo pants and boots, tan shirt and matching baseball cap, Elena knew she resembled a park ranger more than she did a soldier. Even without the words *DOD CIVILIAN* emblazoned across her breast pocket, there was no chance that anyone could mistake her for being military. She certainly wasn't the first civilian to arrive on the base, and yet she couldn't help but feel conspicuous as she walked past the rows of housing. When she drew alongside the Tactical Operations Center where Chase had dressed her down, she couldn't prevent a swift, sideways glance at the windows.

Was he still inside? A part of her wanted to go to him and try to apologize for their earlier altercation. She didn't like being at odds with him, not after what they'd shared. But then she remembered his scathing words, insinuating that she didn't have what it took to live on the base. Tipping her chin up, she strode past the office, her back rigid. She'd show him exactly what she was made of. She might not be a man, and she wasn't military, but she could certainly deal with the conditions here at Sharlana as well as any soldier, female or otherwise.

She stopped in front of a large hangar with a sign out front that read S-4 Supply. Opening the door, she found herself in a cool, dark warehouse with row after row of shelving that reached to the ceiling. Large bins were stacked along the walls, and hundreds of boxes marked with stenciled stock numbers rested on the shelves. Elena could hear the low murmur of masculine voices from the rear of the hangar and cautiously made her way toward them.

A small office had been built in a corner of the warehouse, and through the pass-through window, Elena saw a female soldier sitting at a desk doing paperwork. Seeing Elena, she stood up and leaned through the window, smiling in a friendly way.

"Can I help you, ma'am?"

Elena approached the window. "I hope so—" she broke off to glance at the front of the woman's uniform "—Specialist Ostergard. I was told to come here if I needed any supplies."

"That's right. What do you need?"

"Well, a mattress for starters. And bed linens. I just arrived today."

SPC Ostergard's expression was one of surprise. "You don't have a mattress on your cot?"

"There's a box spring, but no mattress. And no sheets or blankets."

The woman looked quickly away, but Elena could have sworn she was suppressing a smirk. "Ma'am, you do have a mattress."

Elena smiled sweetly back at her. "No, I don't."

"Yes, you do. What you're calling a box spring is actually the mattress."

Elena stared at her in disbelief. "But it's as hard as a rock, and only about four inches thick. How can you call that a mattress?"

"It's standard military issue to every person on this base, ma'am. Maybe you could ask a family member to mail you a foam pad or a mattress topper. That's what most of us do."

Elena blew out an exasperated breath. "Well, what about sheets and blankets?"

"We don't supply those. Everyone just uses their sleeping bag. I'm sorry, that information should have been made clear to you during basic contingency ops training."

Elena digested this, acknowledging silently that she might have missed that bit of information during the stateside orientation. But before she could reply, a voice spoke from behind her.

"What's the problem, Ms. De la Vega? Your living quarters not up to your usual standards?"

Elena whirled around to see Chase and two other soldiers standing several feet away. Chase held a clipboard in one hand, and the soldiers were each pushing a hand truck loaded with supplies they had pulled from the nearby shelves. Elena realized it must have been their voices she'd heard when she'd first entered the hangar. How much of her conversation had Chase overheard? She'd die before she let him know that she'd mistaken her mattress for a box spring, or that she'd actually requested sheets and blankets.

"No," she assured him with a smile. "My living quarters are great. I was just, um, becoming familiar with the base and thought I would check out the supply office."

"Uh-huh." Both his tone and his expression told Elena he wasn't buying her story.

"Actually," she said quickly, "I was wondering where

I might get some soap and shampoo. I left mine back at the hotel in Kuwait."

From the expression on Chase's face, Elena knew he was remembering the previous night. She doubted he had woken up with sore muscles as a result of their nocturnal activities. He was in perfect condition. And what did she really know about him, after all? He might be well accustomed to having one-night stands with complete strangers. The thought darkened her mood, and she found it difficult to maintain her smile as she envisioned him in bed with other women.

Chase turned to the soldiers. "Can you finish up here? I'll walk Ms. De la Vega over to the post exchange."

"Oh, no," Elena protested. "That's really not necessary. I can see you're busy. I can find my way there on my own."

No way did she want to spend any more time alone with Chase, not after their previous confrontation. She wasn't sure she could endure another tongue-lashing from him, at least not without losing her composure and subjecting him to one of her own.

"I insist," Chase said. "Besides, there're a few things I need to pick up myself."

Elena could see that he wouldn't take no for an answer, and there didn't seem any point in arguing further. Reluctantly, she followed him out of the warehouse. Earlier, he'd worn only a T-shirt and shorts. Now he wore standard combat cammies, with a flak vest and an accessory belt weighted down with various pouches and gadgets. He looked as if he'd just stepped off the cover of *Soldier of Fortune* magazine, all broad shoulders and lean hips and badass attitude.

Just seeing him made Elena's pulse quicken and her

stomach flutter. Why did he have to be so *hot?* It would be so much easier to maintain her feminine outrage if she wasn't always thinking about his masculine assets. He seemed taller than he had when she'd met him in Kuwait, and his battle gear made him look more imposing. He pulled a pair of sunglasses out of his vest pocket and slid them on, effectively shielding his eyes from her. Elena found she was actually a little in awe of him. They walked silently for several moments.

"Listen, I want to apologize for what I said earlier." He stopped and faced her. "I was out of line. I was just so—" He paused, obviously struggling for words. "I was shocked to see you, plain and simple."

Elena nodded. "I understand."

"No, I don't think you do. You see, I know what's out there." He stabbed a finger beyond the fencing that surrounded the base, toward the distant mountains. "Hiding in those hills is an enemy who would do anything— *anything*—to destroy us. And while the military on this base are trained to deal with that, you aren't."

Elena tipped her chin up, refusing to be intimidated. She stepped closer and tapped a finger against his body armor. "Well, I guess that's why I have you. To protect me."

To her astonishment, he gripped her by the shoulders and gave her a light shake. "You're not getting it. I can try to protect you, but I'm not always going to be here. My job takes me outside this base for long periods of time. Who's going to protect you then, Elena? Your little guardian-angel necklace?"

She stared at him. She couldn't see his eyes behind the sunglasses, but a muscle worked convulsively in his jaw.

"What makes you think I even need protecting? I already told you, I can take care of myself."

Chase made a growling sound of frustration and before Elena could guess his intent, one hand closed around her upper arm and he hauled her alongside him as he strode down the street. They stopped in front of a concrete structure reinforced on all sides with sandbags. Chase thrust her through the open door and into a concrete tunnel that led downward until they entered a small chamber.

"This is a bomb shelter," Chase said grimly. "If we come under mortar attack, the sirens will go off. You grab your helmet and your vest and you run as fast as you can to this shelter, you got that?"

Elena glanced around at the dark room, feeling claustrophobic despite the open doorway that allowed some light to enter. She nodded, "Yes, I understand."

"You don't stop to grab your pocketbook or your ID card or anything else. You just get your ass in here, understood?"

Elena stared at him. "Yes, I understand. Now let go, you're hurting me."

Chase snatched his sunglasses off and although he loosened his grip, he didn't release her. "I'm dead serious, Elena."

"So am I." She tried to disengage herself, but his fingers were locked around her arm. "Listen, Chase, I appreciate your concern, I really do. But just because we…" She broke off, not sure how to continue and then decided to just be blunt. "You're not responsible for me just because we spent one night together."

"I know that, damn it." He stepped closer, and Elena felt her breath catch at the intensity of his expression.

"But the fact is, whether you like it or not, we have a connection. Don't pretend that you don't know it's true."

They had a connection. Elena's heartbeat quickened and the air changed. She could almost feel the electric charge that crackled between them. But there was no denying that what he said was true. There *was* a connection between them.

"Yes," she finally acknowledged. "I know it's true. But you said yourself that you won't give me any preferential treatment, so why are you doing this?"

"Because I don't want you to rely on anyone else—not the female soldiers you bunk with, and not even me—to help you out if there's an emergency, okay? You need to know exactly what to do without being told and without freaking out."

Elena arched an eyebrow at him. "I assure you that I would not *freak out*."

"Let's hope we never have to find out."

His expression was inscrutable in the hazy light, and Elena was suddenly conscious of the fact that they were alone in the bunker. He was standing close enough that she could actually smell his scent, and it brought all the memories of the previous night rushing back. The feel of his lips. The texture of his skin.

The way he tasted.

"I—I should go," she said, aware of how breathless her voice sounded. Her gaze drifted over his face and lingered on his mouth. He still held her, but now his grip changed. His hand slid down the length of her arm and captured her hand, turning it over and stroking his thumb over her palm.

"So fucking soft," he muttered.

The expression on his face was so sensual that Elena's

breath caught, and she couldn't prevent her fingers from curling around his. "Chase..."

He made a rough sound of defeat and hauled her against his chest as he lowered his head toward hers. Elena had only an instant to register the unyielding surface of his protective vest and the hard jut of his utility belt when a voice interrupted them from outside the bunker.

"Sergeant McCormick, sir! You down here?"

Chase pushed Elena away from him just before a shadow appeared in the entrance to the bunker. The soldier came to an abrupt halt when he saw Elena.

"Sorry, sir," he said in a rush, and Elena saw it was Mike Corrente. "You're needed at tactical. Intel says a large force of Taliban fighters is congregating about six miles down the south road."

The transformation in Chase was immediate and a little alarming to watch. In the space of a heartbeat he went from warm and intimate to cold and professional.

Gripping Elena's elbow, he steered her toward the entrance, his strides long and purposeful. "I'll take my men and use the north road to circle around and position ourselves above them."

Elena had to trot to keep up with Chase as they exited the bunker, and her heart rate kicked up a notch at the thought of him in danger.

"Best we can tell, they're hoping to overrun the compound after nightfall. Charlie Platoon was in the one of the villages outside Spera to pick up this guy who the villagers say has ties with the Taliban. But now they're on their way to intercept these guys."

"Tell them to avoid the wadi," Chase said. "That entire riverbed is an ambush point." He pulled Elena to a halt outside the Tactical Operations Center. "Go back to your living quarters and stay there, understood? Mike'll have someone escort you to the chow hall, and then back to your hut. Under no circumstances are you to leave it without a military escort. And remember what I said. If those sirens go off, you get your ass into that bunker."

Elena nodded. "What about you?"

For just a moment, his face softened and he reached out to stroke her cheek. "Don't worry about me. This is what I do best. Just take care of yourself."

But as he turned and took the stairs to the operations center two at a time, Elena realized she wasn't afraid for herself at all.

All her thoughts were centered on Chase.

The knowledge that he might be killed caused her chest to constrict. She'd told herself that what they'd done hadn't meant anything. They'd been two strangers who had briefly taken pleasure in each other, knowing that such enjoyment might not be available to either of them again for a very long time. Whatever connection they shared went no deeper than a physical attraction. So why, then, did it feel as if he'd taken a part of her with him when he left?

6

"WE'LL JUST COLLECT your roommate and then I'll bring
you both over to the chow hall now," Mike Corrente
said as he and Elena walked swiftly back to her living
quarters. "I'll have one of the engineers walk you back
afterward. I think the orientation brief may have to wait
until tomorrow."

Elena agreed. From the activity surrounding them,
she understood that the troops on the base had more
important things to do than provide a tour to the recently
arrived civilians. They skirted groups of soldiers who
were busy prepping their weapons and shoving their
gear into rucksacks, and the energy level seemed to have
ratcheted through the roof. Elena could almost feel the
excitement of the young men as they prepared to confront
the enemy and realized they were actually looking forward to the encounter. Beyond the housing area, Elena
saw more men loading Humvees and armored vehicles
with weapons and ammo.

"How long will Ch—Sergeant McCormick be gone?"
she finally asked.

The sergeant shrugged. "Hard to say. He and his men

could be gone overnight, or they could be gone for a week."

"What is it that he does, exactly?"

Mike slanted her a quizzical look. "You really don't know? He and his men do recon, and they've actually taken out several key Taliban leaders."

Elena frowned. "But he just arrived this morning, right?"

They'd arrived outside the door to Elena's hut, and the sergeant paused to consider her. "This is McCormick's fourth deployment to this region. His was one of the first special ops teams to be dropped into this zone after the war began. Hell, he helped to establish this as a base when it was little more than a series of mud huts surrounded by stone walls. If anyone knows this region, it's McCormick."

Elena digested this information. She wasn't surprised that Chase was special ops; he oozed confidence and capability. It was just part of who he was, and Elena knew instinctively that she could trust him with her life.

But she also understood that a man who was on his fourth deployment to Afghanistan, after having spent a year in Iraq, was a career military guy. He didn't have the time or luxury for long-term relationships. She couldn't feel bitter about this, since Chase had told her up front that he couldn't offer her anything more than one night.

Now she understood why.

Opening the door to her hut, she saw three female soldiers inside, stuffing gear into their backpacks. The one nearest the door gave her a brief nod. She looked to be in her early twenties, with a freckled face and pale blue eyes.

"Ma'am," she said in way of acknowledgment, and bent back to her task.

The other two soldiers were slightly older, and they barely glanced up as Elena entered. At the far end of the hut, Sylvia sat on her bed watching them, her eyes wide with apprehension.

"Hey, Sylvia," Elena called. "Sergeant Corrente is going to bring us over to the chow hall."

One of the soldiers, a pretty girl with dark eyes and hair, looked up when Elena mentioned Sergeant Corrente. Her gaze moved beyond Elena to the door and without a word, she stood up and slung her pack over her shoulder. Squeezing past Elena, she left the hut.

"Perfect," muttered the other woman, shoving a pair of socks deep into her rucksack. "We'll be lucky if we get out of here today. Once those two catch sight of each other, nothing else matters."

The freckle-faced girl laughed. "Yep, got that right. Poor Mike. He doesn't know whether to be pissed off that Valerie got assigned to the same base as himself, or get down on his knees and thank his lucky stars."

The first woman snorted. "He'll be pissed until the first time she gets him alone and rocks his world. Then he'll be thanking his lucky stars."

Her interest piqued, Elena stepped into her little cubby and pretended to be absorbed unpacking her duffel bags. In reality, it took all her self-restraint not to peek out the window to see what was happening with Sergeant Corrente and the girl named Valerie.

She looked at Sylvia, who hadn't moved.

"Sylvia? Hey, you okay?"

"I think your friend is freaked out over the news that the Taliban is closing in," said the freckled-faced woman, extending a hand toward Elena. She spoke in a soft, Southern accent. "I'm Corporal Callie Linden. I told her it's no big deal, but I don't think she believes me."

"I'm Elena de la Vega." Elena frowned as the woman stood up. "You're not actually going out there to confront the Taliban, are you?"

"I'm a gunner, ma'am. If they send a convoy out, then I'll go with them." She jerked her head in the direction of the third woman. "Corporal Chapman here does house-to-house searches with the guys because only female soldiers can perform body searches of the local women." She shrugged. "Like I said, it's no big deal."

Elena hesitated. "What you said about your friend and Sergeant Corrente..."

"Val and Mike? What about them?"

"I know it's none of my business, but were you referring to them having, you know, sex?"

Callie grinned. "Val's been plotting to get that boy alone since she first laid eyes on him, and I don't think he'll put up too much of a fight."

"Okay, I know this sounds stupid, but I was told in no uncertain terms that sex is strictly forbidden. Is that true?"

The first woman, Corporal Chapman, gave a hoot of laughter. "They can try to forbid it, but it's happening whether the brass likes it or not. General Order One doesn't expressly prohibit having sex, but it's highly discouraged. Yeah, there are rules about how we're supposed to behave, like we're not supposed to be in each other's quarters with the door closed." She gave another snort. "Like that's going to deter anyone. Believe me, if two people want sex, they'll find a way."

"Those rules," Elena ventured. "Do they apply to *everyone?*"

Corporal Chapman sharpened her attention on Elena. "Why do you ask? Do you have your eye on one of our boys already?"

Elena couldn't prevent the heat that washed into her face. "Of course not. I was just wondering."

"Uh-huh. Sure." But when it became clear that Elena wasn't about to offer anything more, she shrugged. "Even if the rules don't apply to you, they apply to the soldier you're fantasizing about. But like I said, if two people want to be together badly enough, they'll find a way. We always have female soldiers turning up pregnant and trust me, they didn't get that way by themselves."

Elena watched as the women finished stowing their gear and left the building, before turning her attention back to Sylvia. She sat on the edge of her bed, twisting her blanket in her thin fingers.

"Hey, what's going on?" Elena asked gently. "There's nothing to be afraid of. We're protected by some of the best and bravest soldiers in the world." She adopted a brisk, friendly tone. "C'mon, let's go get something to eat. Personally, I'm starving."

But Sylvia only shook her head. "No, I couldn't eat a thing. My stomach is in knots. I think I'll just stay here."

Elena nodded in sympathy. "All right. I'll bring something back for you, then. Why don't you lie down and try to get some rest? I'll be back soon, I promise."

Sylvia nodded and at Elena's urging, lay woodenly

on the bed with her eyes open, as if she expected the Taliban to burst through the door at any moment.

Elena left the hut and stopped uncertainly when she saw Mike Corrente in a heated, hushed conversation with the dark-haired woman who had left their living quarters so abruptly. Mike wore an expression of extreme frustration and twin patches of color rode high on his cheekbones. Valerie looked defiant. As Elena closed the door behind her, both soldiers looked up, and while Mike was distracted, Valerie took the opportunity to turn and walk away. For a brief instant, Elena was certain that Mike would go after her, before he visibly restrained himself.

"Where's Ms. Dobbs?" he asked in a clipped tone.

"Not feeling well. Look, if you just want to point me in the right direction, I can find my own way to the chow hall."

"No doing," he answered, shaking his head. "I promised McCormick I wouldn't let you go anywhere alone and I don't intend to."

Elena sighed. "Fine. Let's go."

As they made their way through the housing area and past the latrines and showers, Elena was amazed at the level of activity on the base. The sound of diesel engines filled the air as a dozen Humvees and armored vehicles prepared to leave the base and patrol the surrounding area. Two helicopters stood on the landing strip, the downward wash of their rotors creating small sandstorms of dust that rolled across the base in billowing clouds.

Elena wondered what Chase was doing at that moment. Had he and his team already left the base? Were they making their way toward the spot where the Taliban forces had been spotted? She knew for a fact that he hadn't slept the previous night; would he get any sleep this night? Her mind whirled with all the possible scenarios. Her stomach was a knot of anxiety, and she didn't think she'd be able to eat.

"Here we are." The sergeant's voice interrupted her thoughts. They had arrived at the chow hall, and the delicious aroma of grilled burgers and French fries made her mouth water. Inside, rows of tables and benches filled a large room.

"Just grab a tray and move through the line," Mike instructed, nodding toward the hot food. "There's also a salad bar and a dessert bar and the drinks are over there. You can pretty much help yourself to whatever you want, as much as you want."

Elena stared around her, amazed by the selection. "I thought I'd be eating MREs," she marveled, referring to the prepackaged field rations that the military used in combat.

Mike smiled. "No way. We're the best-fed military in the world." He winked at her and patted his flat stomach. "The only problem is the food is almost too good."

Although it had seemed to Elena that every able-bodied person on the base was gearing up to confront the enemy, the dining area was about half-filled with people, both military and civilian. She saw several of the men who had flown in on the same helicopter with her, and one of them raised a hand in friendly acknowledgement.

Not feeling particularly sociable, Elena smiled but turned to Mike. "I'm just going to grab something and bring it back to my room. You don't need to wait."

Planting his feet apart, Mike crossed his arms. "That's okay, ma'am. I'll wait."

Giving him a dubious look, Elena nodded. "Fine. I'll be right back."

She quickly chose some sandwiches, fruit and bottled drinks and bundled them all in a paper bag. Despite Mike's determination to wait for her, she sensed that he was anxious to get back to his job.

The sun was setting behind the mountains as they made their way back toward the living quarters, and Elena could feel the temperature beginning to drop.

"Does it get cold here at night?" she asked.

"It can. We're in the desert, so the difference between day and night is pretty extreme. Best to wear layers, since you never can tell what the weather will do." He hesitated before continuing. "So, um, how're your living quarters working out?"

Elena shrugged. "I grew up with two sisters so I'm sort of used to sharing my space."

"Did you—did you meet the enlisted women?"

Elena glanced sharply at him. "Do you mean Valerie?"

To her amazement, twin spots of ruddy color appeared on his cheeks. "Yeah. She won't tell me if she's going out on patrol, or not. Thinks I'll freak out, or something."

"I don't know about Valerie, but the other two women said they were most likely going out."

They were approaching Elena's housing unit when they heard a shrill, terrified scream from inside. Elena barely had time to register what was happening before Mike broke into a run and flung the door to her hut open, disappearing inside. Elena followed, her heart hammering. She reached the open doorway and peered over Mike's shoulder to see Sylvia standing on top of her bed, an expression of horror on her pale face. She stabbed a finger toward the floor.

"There! Did you see it? Under the bed! It went under the bed!"

Mike worked his way through the cubicles, crouching down to check the floor as he went. "What is it? What am I looking for? A snake? A scorpion?"

"Sp-spider," Sylvia managed in a choked voice. "A huge spider."

"Damn," Mike muttered. "I hate frickin' spiders."

Elena stood in the doorway, poised to run, when she saw a dark shape, easily as big as her hand, scuttle across the floor. Only scuttle was the wrong word, because that would imply the thing merely hurried, when in reality it *raced* across the open floor. Directly toward her.

Elena couldn't help herself. She shrieked and flung herself outside, her eyes scanning the ground in case the thing actually decided to follow her. She was only vaguely aware of several soldiers running in her direction, and from inside the hut, Sylvia squealing in fright.

Strong hands gripped her by the upper arms and gave her a slight shake. "Elena, what's wrong? Are you all right?"

"Spider," she managed to gasp as Chase stared down at her. "A huge spider!"

"Wait here," he said grimly and ducked inside the housing unit.

Elena leaned back against the wall of the hut, listening to the chaotic noises coming from inside. It sounded as if they were overturning the beds in their search for the enormous creature. She could just distinguish Chase's voice speaking in low tones, presumably to calm Sylvia.

She jumped when Mike emerged from the hut, looking a little stunned.

"Ah, you might want to move away a little," he said when he saw Elena standing beside the door.

There was a collective gasp from the congregated soldiers as Chase emerged from the hut. Dangling from his gloved hand was a massive spider.

Elena recoiled in horror.

"It's okay," he assured her. "It can't hurt you now."

"Oh, my god," she breathed, staring at the creature in disbelief. "What is it?"

"The soldiers call these camel spiders."

"Is it alive?"

Before Chase could answer, the thing made a hideous noise and began to twitch in his hand. As one, the soldiers took a step backward.

"Damn, Sergeant," one man said, "you're either the bravest son of a bitch I've ever seen or the dumbest."

Chase held the spider up and considered it. "They're actually not venomous. This guy was probably just looking for a shady place to hide."

The spider was sand-colored and hairy, and each of its legs were easily six inches long. It jerked grotesquely in Chase's hand. Elena shuddered and looked away, repulsed by the thing. Her imagination conjured up horrible images of what might have happened had Chase not captured it. What if the spider had attacked her during the night?

"Somebody get me a box or a jar," Chase commanded. He turned to Elena. "You okay?"

She couldn't understand how he could be so calm while holding something so frightening. "I don't think

I can go back in there," she said, indicating her sleeping quarters. "What if there are more?"

"We checked everything and the hut is clear. There's nothing in there to be afraid of."

Elena gave a disbelieving snort. "Right. You couldn't pay me enough money to sleep in there."

A corner of Chase's mouth lifted and his eyes gleamed with humor. "I did warn you that the conditions here are different than what you're accustomed to."

She bristled. "If you even try to insinuate that I'm acting like a typical female, Chase, then take a good look around. Even your own soldiers are afraid to get near that thing." She grimaced. "Any human should be afraid to get near something that revolting."

Chase laughed. "Okay, I concede."

One of the soldiers came forward with a cardboard box, and Chase dropped the spider inside, quickly closing the top before it could escape. He handed the box back to the soldier. "Release it outside the wire."

The soldier blanched. "Me?"

Chase arched an eyebrow. "You have a particular problem, Corporal, that prevents you from releasing an insect?"

The man flushed and defiantly snatched the box from Chase's hands, although Elena noted how he held it at arm's length. "No, sir," he snapped. "No problem."

He strode away, and Chase turned to the remaining men. "Okay, show's over. Back to your posts."

"Speaking of which," Elena said quietly, "why aren't you at your post? Something about insurgents preparing to overrun the compound? What are you doing here? I thought you were against rescuing damsels in distress."

He glanced at her. "The intel was false," he said curtly.

"Ah. Well, that's a relief. I mean, if you'd been gone, who would have captured that little critter?" Elena peered into the hut to see Sylvia still standing on her bed, her face pale. "The spider is gone," she assured the other woman. "You can come down."

Sylvia gingerly climbed from the bed and came outside. Elena could see she was shaking. She held out the bag she'd carried from the dining facility. "I brought you a sandwich and something to drink."

Sylvia grimaced. "Thanks, but I couldn't eat a thing." She drew in a shaky breath and faced Chase. "Actually, I'd like to speak with whoever is in charge of the DPA folks."

Chase's expression didn't change. "That would be Colonel Vinson. I can walk you to his office, if you'd like."

Realization hit Elena, and she reached out to touch Sylvia's shoulder. "You can't leave. Not when you've just gotten here."

Sylvia turned around. "I can't stay. I'm sorry, but I completely underestimated what the conditions would be like out here." She glanced back into the hut and Elena saw a shudder go through her. "I can't sleep in there, or anyplace else where there might be those spiders. Or worse. I'm sorry."

"There's nothing to be sorry about," Chase assured her. "You're making the right choice."

Elena briefly narrowed her eyes at him before turning back to the older woman. "Sylvia, you don't have to do this. Granted, the spider was disgusting, but it wasn't poisonous. We really need you out here. The *troops* really need you here. I wish you'd reconsider."

Sylvia shook her head. "I can't. I'm going to ask if I can leave on the next helicopter out."

Reluctantly, Elena glanced at Chase. She fully expected to see an expression of triumph on his face, but his features were somber as he considered Sylvia. "I'll personally ensure that you're on a flight back to Kuwait first thing tomorrow." He shifted his attention to Elena. "Can I persuade you to go with her, Ms. De la Vega?"

"Not a chance."

"Fine," he said, clearly not pleased. "But next time there's an uninvited, eight-inch critter in your bed, don't expect the cavalry to come to your rescue."

Elena smiled sweetly and allowed her gaze to drift over him. "Trust me. The next time I have an eight-inch critter in my bed, it won't be uninvited."

7

ELENA SPENT a sleepless night tossing and turning on
her hard pallet, and she knew Sylvia did the same. After
the other woman had returned from Colonel Vinson's
office, she'd confirmed that she would be leaving in the
morning. Then she had repacked her duffel bags with
the items she'd unpacked just hours before, and had slid
fully clothed into her sleeping bag. The female soldiers
didn't return that night, and it was just Elena and Sylvia
in the hut. The temperatures fell and Elena shivered in
her sleeping bag, her eyes wide open.

The base apparently didn't sleep, either. Elena listened to the sound of diesel engines throbbing to life,
and the shouts of soldiers as they went about their work.
She dragged the sleeping bag up over her shoulders and
turned onto her side, thinking about the events of the
day. Part of her understood why Chase wanted her to
go home, but another part of her felt hurt and insulted
by his eagerness to see her gone. She still had a difficult
time reconciling the man she'd known in Kuwait with the
hard-eyed soldier here in Afghanistan. She just wished
she knew if his desire to send her home really had to

do with her safety or his own discomfort at having her around.

She had just begun to drift off when a strident alarm snapped her into full awareness. Sylvia mumbled something incoherent and Elena heard her fumbling in the dark until finally, she hit the alarm and blissful silence ensued. But for Elena, there was no falling asleep.

With a groan, she sat up and pushed the sleeping bag back, shivering in the cool air. Reaching out, she groped for the light attached to the wall and snapped it on, illuminating her little sleeping compartment. She looked over at Sylvia, who was also sitting up and rubbing her eyes.

"What time is it?" Elena asked.

"About 4:00 a.m. Sergeant Corrente is coming to get me in ten minutes to bring me to the airstrip." Sylvia swung her legs over the edge of her bed and scrubbed her hands over her face. "God, I'm tired."

Elena agreed. She was exhausted to her very bones, but she knew she'd never be able to get back to sleep. "I think I'll go grab a shower and something to eat, and then head over to the contracting center," she announced. "Any chance I can borrow your shampoo?"

Leaning over, Sylvia unzipped her duffel bag and tossed Elena a small cosmetic kit. "You can keep it," she said. "I'm not going to need it."

Elena slid her feet into her boots. "Well, I guess this is it," she said to Sylvia. "I'm sorry this didn't work out for you."

Sylvia gave a huff of laughter. "I'm not. I'm glad I came, if only for the fact that I now realize how lucky I am."

"What do you mean?"

Sylvia shrugged and looked a little embarrassed. "I've spent the past year feeling sorry for myself. My whole life changed after my husband left me. Somehow, I believed that was a bad thing." She looked around the room they shared. "But coming over here and seeing how these young people live was a real wake-up call. They work in these horrible conditions, far away from their loved ones, and yet I haven't heard one complaint. It's a little humbling."

Elena knew exactly what she meant. She considered that this was Chase's fourth deployment to Afghanistan and that he was prepared to spend another year away from his family.

"It does make you reconsider what your priorities are," she agreed. "I'm sure none of these soldiers take what they have for granted, not when they know they could lose everything at any time. You figure out really quick what it is that you care about."

She wondered what Chase cared about. Who were his loved ones? He'd told her that he wasn't married, but did he have someone waiting for him at home? She realized she knew next to nothing about the man, other than the fact he was from North Carolina. If circumstance hadn't placed them on the same outpost together, she would never have seen him again, never known anything more about him than what she'd learned during that one amazing night.

The thought was oddly depressing.

Bending down, she unzipped her duffel bag to pull out a clean change of clothing and a towel, when something white fell from the folds of fabric and drifted to the floor. Elena picked up a slip of paper that had been folded in half, her name scrawled across the front. Her pulse quickened as she slowly opened the note, half afraid of what she might find. He'd only written two lines, but they were enough for Elena.

Didn't want to wake you up, but not ready to say goodbye.
Write to me, Elena.

He'd provided an e-mail address, and his signature was a bold slash of ink across the bottom of the note. The message was so much like him, direct and authoritative, that she had to smile.

He hadn't wanted to say goodbye.

The realization that he'd wanted to stay in touch with her caused a slow warmth to seep through her. She closed her fingers over the paper. *Write to me, Elena.* Which meant that his earlier hostility at seeing her on the base was from his own fears for her safety, and not because he didn't want her around.

"Elena, are you sure you want to stay here for six months?" Sylvia's voice interrupted her thoughts. "There's room on that helicopter for you if you think you'd like to go home."

Elena turned to the other woman with a smile. "Oh, no. I'm definitely going to stay. In fact, I'm really looking forward to it. But thanks."

She gave Sylvia a brief hug and then hefted her backpack over her shoulder. Stepping outside into the cool darkness of predawn, she made her way to the lavatory facilities, but her thoughts were on Chase. He'd written the note believing he wouldn't see her again, at least not so soon. But the fact that he'd given her his e-mail address and asked her to write to him was huge. She knew instinctively that he wasn't the kind of guy to give his personal information out lightly.

Lost in her thoughts, she made her way past the other living quarters. The base was mostly quiet at this hour, although she could hear the lazy *thwap-thwap* of an idling helicopter over on the landing pad, and guessed it was Sylvia's ride home.

She entered the showers and saw a row of changing stalls facing a wall of lockers. Beyond the locker room, she could hear the spray of water from the shower room itself, which meant she wasn't going to have the privacy she'd hoped for. With a resigned sigh, she set her belongings in the closest stall and quickly undressed. Wrapping her towel around her, she grabbed the bottle of shampoo that Sylvia had given to her and padded over to the open shower room.

And stopped dead in her tracks.

A man stood beneath the spray of a single nozzle, steam wreathing his body. A supremely muscled, supremely naked man.

Chase.

All the saliva in Elena's mouth evaporated at the sight of him. He stood with his back to her, his head bent as water sluiced down his body. He soaped himself, his hands moving over his chest and up under his arms, washing there before sliding lower, over his stomach. He was golden everywhere except for the paler skin of his hips and buttocks. Despite having seen him unclothed before, Elena greedily drank in the sight of him.

He was the most gorgeous man she'd ever seen, lean and hard, and his face…with his cheekbones and full, sensual mouth, he had a face that could make an angel weep. Elena just stood there, clutching her towel and staring. She couldn't drag her gaze away from him, devouring the play of muscles along his sleek back. His ass was perfect, his thighs hard and sinewy. She remembered all too well the feel of them between her own, and a hot burst of yearning spread through her abdomen.

He tipped his head back, exposing his strong throat and letting the spray hit him full in the face before he slicked it away with one hand. He turned slightly, and Elena saw the heavy thrust of his penis; he was semi-aroused. Heat swamped her, churning through her veins and making her feel a little light-headed.

The plastic bottle of shampoo slipped from her fingers and bounced on the tiled floor. His head snapped around and in the next instant their gazes collided. Elena couldn't move, couldn't breathe. Chase's eyes turned hot, and even from where she stood, she could see how every muscle in his body tightened at the sight of her, and his erection went from halfhearted to rampant in the space of a heartbeat. Her breathing quickened and with a mumbled apology, she turned on wobbly legs to flee.

"Elena." He moved fast. He caught her by the arm and spun her around, and she found herself hauled against his wet chest. Steam still rose from his skin in a fine mist, and his lashes were spiky with moisture.

"Elena," he said hoarsely. "What are you doing in here?"

She stared at him, mesmerized by the hunger in his expression. "I came to take a shower," she breathed.

"This is the men's shower. You can't be in here."

The sound of voices drifted toward them from outside the door. Glancing swiftly around, Chase dragged her into a changing stall and jerked the curtain closed.

Before Elena could protest, he lifted her onto the wooden bench and covered her mouth with his fingers, silencing her with a single look.

"Sergeant McCormick, you in here, sir?"

Elena recognized the voice as Pete Cleary's.

"Uh, yeah," Chase called back. His voice was rough.

"I just thought you should know the helo's taking off, but your girl's not on board."

His girl.

Elena didn't have to guess who Pete referred to, and her eyes snapped back to Chase's over the warmth of his hand. He was watching her intently, and twin patches of ruddy color rode high on his chiseled cheekbones. His eyes glittered, more green than hazel, and his breath came in short pants. He had a small, perfect mole on his collarbone and as Elena watched, a droplet of water fell from his hair and landed just above it, before trickling downward in a tiny rivulet. Her eyes followed its path, and she had an overwhelming desire to lap at the moisture with her tongue.

"Sir?"

Elena heard heavy footsteps enter the shower room.

"I understand. Thank you, Corporal," Chase finally responded. "I'll be out shortly."

The footsteps receded and Chase slowly removed his hand from her mouth. Standing on the bench, Elena towered over him. She realized her hands were resting on his broad shoulders, and her fingers spread across his skin almost reflexively. Her glance swept downward and she was reminded he was still naked, and still very much aroused. Beneath the towel, her nipples contracted. She moistened her lips.

"I thought this was the women's shower," she whispered, half in explanation, half in apology.

"Elena," he groaned, and his fingers tightened on her waist, bunching in the terry cloth and dragging it downward until the towel fell away and cool air wafted over her bare breasts and stomach.

She watched, entranced, as his eyes darkened. Then he leaned forward and very gently circled his hot tongue around one nipple. Elena gasped and her hands crept upward to clutch his head, her fingers burrowing into his dripping hair. He drew her breast into his mouth and suckled her, while his big hands cupped her bottom and pulled her closer, until she leaned fully into him.

He sucked harder and from between her thighs came an answering throb, sharp and sweet. He kneaded her bottom, and then his fingers dipped between her buttocks and found the secret spot where she pulsed hotly. He touched her intimately, one finger probing her slick entrance until Elena groaned and her legs buckled.

"Hold on to me," he said, his voice husky, before he crouched in front of her and began laving her with his mouth and tongue.

Elena groaned. Part of her knew she should stop him, but she was too far gone. Her blood pounded hot and insistent through her veins, until she thought she might spontaneously combust. She threaded her fingers through his wet hair, and when he urged her thighs farther apart, she complied, rolling her head back against the wall of the changing stall. She was completely unrestrained in her urgency; the part of her brain that still functioned understood that an entire platoon of U.S. Marines could come marching through the shower room at any moment.

She didn't care.

All that mattered was the man who knelt before her, pleasuring her with his hands and tongue. She glanced down and the sight of his dark head at the juncture of her thighs, combined with the erotic sensations he created, was too much. She gave a strangled cry as her orgasm crashed through her. Even then, Chase didn't stop, drawing her pleasure out until she thought she couldn't take any more and still survive. Her fingers were still tangled in his hair, and she didn't let go, even when he worked his way up her body, pressing warm, moist kisses along her heaving stomach and breasts. When he finally stood upright, he cupped her face in his big hands and slanted his mouth hard across hers, kissing her deeply. Elena could taste her own essence on his lips.

She wreathed her arms around his neck, boneless with release, and kissed him back. "Now it's your turn," she breathed into his mouth. She could feel him, hot and hard against her thighs, but as she slid a hand down to touch him, he captured her wrist, halting her.

"You have to go," he muttered. "Someone could come in."

Elena drew back just enough to search his eyes, but his expression was shuttered. "I don't *have* to go," she protested softly. "Not if you don't want me to. I could stay. I *want* to stay."

With a low sound of frustration, he stepped back and reached into a backpack that was on the floor, dragging out a pair of black boxer briefs and pulling them on in quick, jerky motions. Elena slid down the wall until she was sitting on the bench. She watched him fish through his gear until he found a T-shirt and hauled it over his head, yanking it into place.

"You're upset." She picked her towel up and covered herself with it, feeling exposed and vulnerable and defensive. "You were the one who dragged me in here, remember?" she said tightly. "I was leaving."

His head snapped up and his eyes blazed. "Listen, it was fun but it's not going to happen again."

Elena stared at him. The sexual buzz she felt from her orgasm was fading fast, to be replaced with a sense of confusion and the beginnings of a simmering anger. "Oh, that's right. I remember now—no sex on the base. Right?" Chase didn't answer, but she knew from the rigid set of his shoulders that she'd hit the mark. He had laid down the law and nothing would induce him to break it. "So that's how it's going to be, huh?" she continued, boiling. "Everything on your terms? You make the rules and I'm just supposed to obey them?"

"Damn right."

"Well, you can forget it. You're not the boss of me. I do what I want."

It was a childish retort, she knew, but the man infuriated her. He made her do and say things that were totally out of character for her. She'd always prided herself on maintaining her composure, but he completely upset her equilibrium.

Before she could guess his intent, he pinned her against the wall, his face inches from hers. "What, you think this is a *game?*"

Elena refused to be intimidated. "What am I supposed to think? One minute you're telling me that sex is strictly forbidden, and the next you're—you're—"

"Like I said, it was a mistake," he grumbled, releasing her shoulders. His voice was full of self-disgust. "This whole thing was my fault, not yours."

"What a relief. I feel so much better." Elena stood up, but the changing stall was so cramped that it brought her into full body contact with Chase. He flattened himself against the opposite wall as if she carried some contagious disease.

"Don't worry," she said with false sweetness, wrapping her towel around herself and securing it tightly over her breasts. "I'm not going to touch you." She let her gaze drop with deliberation to his crotch, where the fabric of his boxers molded to the impressive outline of his erection.

He still wanted her.

The knowledge pleased her. She knew what self-denial felt like; she'd spent most of her life denying her own desires and impulses. She wanted him to suffer, at least a little. "As much as I'd like to help you out, this looks like a problem you'll need to, uh, handle yourself."

Without waiting for a response, she yanked back the curtain of the tiny stall and stalked out. She paused only long enough to snatch up her own belongings, clutching them against her chest. Without waiting to see if he would follow, she made her way blindly toward the exit, where she saw the women's showers were directly next door.

She just managed to dump her stuff on a bench and turn the shower on before her tough-girl facade crumbled. Stepping beneath the spray, Elena turned her face into the water. She was close to tears. Even when she'd found Larry with that woman, she hadn't felt as miserable as she did right now. Then again, she'd never wanted Larry the way that she wanted First Sergeant Chase Mc-

Cormick. And she'd known Chase for just two days, so what did that say about her?

She'd thought she could have him for just one night, with no inhibitions, no complications and no regrets. And no chance of ever running into him again.

She'd been shocked to find they were both assigned to the same forward operating base, but had convinced herself that she could handle it. On some level, she'd even understood that his initial hostility toward her stemmed from his own concern for her safety. The knowledge had made her feel…special.

But now she had to acknowledge that they had no real relationship. What they had was purely physical, and now it seemed that Chase didn't even want that. She shouldn't feel so upset. She didn't even know the guy, so what did she care if he rejected her? He was probably a Class-A jerk, anyway. One of those arrogant, know-it-all alpha males who believed a woman's place was in the bedroom.

Which, if she was honest with herself, was where she wanted to be.

In *his* bedroom, in *his* bed.

Elena told herself again that the last thing she needed was the complication of a serious relationship, especially out here.

So why did she feel so disappointed?

8

TWO DAYS HAD PASSED since the shower incident. Two days in which Chase had studiously avoided going anywhere on the base where he might cross paths with Elena. If he closed his eyes, he could still see her face as he'd pushed her away from him. He'd hurt her. But Christ, what did she expect? That they'd be able to pick up where they'd left off? The worst part of it was, he desperately wanted to resume their relationship.

He'd known when he'd met her in Kuwait that she was the kind of woman he'd like to know better. Now he told himself that they both had a job to do, and he wouldn't let his libido get in the way of either of them doing that. But he wasn't able to ignore her. The base was too small not to know where she was and what she was doing at any given time.

She'd reported to the contracting center the morning that he'd found her in the men's shower. He'd watched as the contracting officer, Brad Carrington, gave her a tour of the base and took her out to view the waste water treatment facility. They'd spent about an hour talking with the men working on the project, until Carrington had walked her over to the dining facility, and then back to the contracting center.

Carrington was a good-looking guy, and he'd been at the base for over six months. He was career Navy and he was married. But Chase knew that didn't matter to some guys. He wondered if Carrington had tried to put the moves on Elena yet, and his gut twisted at the thought of her with the young officer.

As much as he'd tried, he couldn't stop thinking about that encounter in the showers. She'd been so hot. So incredibly sexy. He'd been unable to sleep, partly due to the time-zone change but mostly because he'd been thinking about her. So he'd risen before dawn and walked over to the showers, but even the cold water hadn't diminished his body's response to his memories of their night together. Then suddenly, there she was. In the shower room, her eyes turning from warm caramel to liquid amber as she'd devoured him.

He might have let her go if Corporal Cleary hadn't threatened to walk in on them. He'd lifted her onto the bench so that if the other man did come in, he'd see just one pair of feet beneath the curtain of the changing area. But that had put him on eye-level with her lush breasts, barely concealed beneath the terry cloth, and her skin had been so smooth and fragrant, and the heat in her eyes had been an invitation he couldn't resist. And the way she'd tasted...

"McCormick, did you hear a word that I just said?"

Chase snapped his attention to the two men who occupied the tactical ops room with him. Staff Sergeant Sean Brody stood next to an oversize map of the Paktika province, circling areas where the Taliban was suspected of having strongholds. He paused, hand poised over the map as a third man, Gunnery Sergeant Rafael Delgado, leaned back in his chair and considered Chase with barely concealed impatience. With his Antonio Banderas curly black hair, dark eyes and growth of beard, Rafe could easily pass for a local tribesman, which made him invaluable for the missions they conducted. More importantly, he spoke both Pashto and Dari, as well as half a dozen other languages. Now he looked at Chase, irritation written all over his face.

"What?" Chase asked, feigning ignorance.

Rafe snorted. "I knew it. You haven't been listening to a fucking thing we've said for the past fifteen minutes."

Chase frowned and pinched the bridge of his nose. As part of a five-man special operations team, he'd worked with Sean and Rafe on more missions than he cared to recall, both in Iraq and Afghanistan. He'd trust either man with his life, and he owed it to them to get his head back in the game and focus on their next operation. He squinted at the map.

"I'm listening," he lied. "We know that Mullah Abdul Raqid is rumored to be using the town of Surobi as his stronghold, but he has the locals so completely terrorized that none of the tribal leaders will give him up for fear of reprisals."

Sean tapped the map. "Until yesterday. Our guys were on patrol along the wadi, here, when they were approached by a local boy. His father had been injured in a fall and was airlifted to a hospital in Kabul."

"And?"

Rafe leaned forward. "And he was supposed to deliver a cache of weapons to Raqid, but now that's not going to happen. None of the other men will go without him, and he's afraid that Raqid will retaliate by coming after his family. He's asked us to protect them."

Chase knew the facts; he'd read the intel report. He and his team already had an approximate location for where Raqid and his men were hiding in the hills above Surobi. But those mountains were pockmarked with caves and crevasses, and Raqid could be in any one of them. Even with an approximate location it would take weeks or months to pinpoint the bastard's exact location. But with the information about the weapons transfer, they had a real shot at finally getting him. The special ops team would move into position, and when the local tribesmen delivered the weapons, Chase and his men would intercept the transfer and, with luck, capture Raqid. In return, the villagers would get a new school and a clinic, paid for with U.S. funds.

"We'll leave in three days. The recon team is already in place, watching the exchange point," Sean said. "We'll insert here," he tapped the map, "and work our way across this mountain range to approach from the rear. Once we're inserted, we'll have just eight hours to get into position."

Chase surveyed the map, noting the rough topography they would have to traverse. They'd managed worse, and so long as their position wasn't betrayed, there was no reason to believe the mission wouldn't be a success. If they succeeded in bringing down Raqid, they would eliminate much of the threat in the local area. Without Raqid, his followers would have a tougher time regrouping. The U.S. troops would ensure that they didn't retaliate against the villagers.

The door exploded open in a cloud of dust and heat,

and a man entered, sweeping the room with a cheerful grin. "Yo, whazzup?"

"Jesus, don't you ever do anything quietly?" Rafe asked, annoyed.

"What, were you sleeping or something, Gunny?" the man asked innocently, but his blue eyes sparkled.

As the newest and youngest member of the special ops team, Corporal Josh Legatowicz, or Lego as the team called him, was far more cocky than he had a right to be. But his personality was so engaging and his skill with a sniper rifle so flawless that the older members of the team put up with him.

"You're late," Sean said, looking pointedly at his watch. "I specifically said to be here at 1300 hours."

Lego grabbed a chair and spun it around, straddling it as he polished an apple against his jacket front and then bit into it with a loud crunch. "Sorry, I got held up. Hey, Sarge," he said, addressing Chase. "Any chance I can do a security detail tomorrow?"

Security details weren't something the special ops team routinely participated in, unless it was for somebody very important, like a general or a diplomat. The Tac Ops received a situation report every six hours, and Chase didn't recall that anyone was scheduled to visit the base.

"What kind of security detail?" he asked.

Lego's grin widened. "A most excellent female civilian needs to drive out to the drilling site, and I just thought it would be safer if she were accompanied by someone who could protect her. Someone like me."

Chase knew he was glowering, but he couldn't help himself. "This *most excellent* female wouldn't be Elena de la Vega by any chance, would it?" But he already knew the answer.

Lego brightened. "Ah, her reputation precedes her. That's awesome. And if you've seen her, then you know what I said is true." He tucked the chair under his armpits as he leaned forward. "Man, this chick isn't just desert hot, you know? She's the real deal. Even if I was back in the States, I'd try to nail her. I give her two weeks before she realizes she can't live without me."

Desert hot was a derogatory term used by the troops to describe female soldiers who achieved a certain level of hotness simply because they were female, and not because they were exceptionally attractive. At home, these women might not have earned a second glance from most guys; here in the desert, they were often the cause of intense rivalry between their male counterparts.

"You're not going to pull security detail for her," Chase said easily. "In fact, you're not going to accompany her anywhere."

"Why not, Sarge?" Lego asked. His face expressed both dismay and disappointment.

"Yeah, why not?" asked Sean, smirking.

"Because she's not leaving the base, that's why,' Chase shot back.

Rafe frowned. "Now wait a minute, McCormick. First of all, she doesn't work for you. Second of all, you can't keep her from doing her job."

"She can damn well do her job from inside the fence," he retorted. "What reason does she have to go out to the drilling site? She's a desk jockey, not an engineer. Seeing the project isn't going to enable her to do her job better, and I'm not about to give up one of my men to accompany her on a nonessential mission."

"That's not your call, McCormick. Besides, the previous contract administrator visited the construction sites fairly regularly." Rafe paused. "But then, the last contract administrator was a man. And that's the crux of the whole issue, isn't it? You don't want her going because she's female."

"I don't want her going because we don't need anybody on this base taking unnecessary risks. I don't care if they're male, female or an alien from outer space. And for the record, the last contract administrator was sent home two weeks ago because he suffered a heart attack, which is why Ms. De la Vega was sent here to replace him. She doesn't need the added stress of visiting the construction site."

Even as he said it, Chase knew he was full of shit. Worse, his team knew it, too. But they were too well trained to let their skepticism show on their faces, and they tactfully said nothing. Except Lego, who hadn't yet figured out when to keep his mouth shut.

"Well, jeez, Sarge, she sure looks healthy to me. But that's all the more reason I should go with her," he argued. "As long as she's with me, she won't be at risk. I'll guard her with my life. And it's not like I have anything else to do, at least not until we move out." He followed this with another of his signature grins that made him look about twelve years old. But Chase knew better. The kid was a total chick magnet.

He also knew he had no valid reason not to let Elena leave the base. The construction site was a scant two miles outside the fence, and was as well guarded as the compound itself. Civilian contractors who were assigned to Sharlana traveled to the site without incident. There was no reason to think that Elena would be in any danger. And as much as he hated to admit it, he had little control over what she did in the normal course of her job—if she wanted to visit the drilling site, he couldn't prevent her from going. But he could damned well make it unpleasant for her.

"I'll go with her," he finally said.

"Yeah, you look real reluctant about it, too," Rafe said sardonically. "I can see it's the last thing in the world you want to do."

"Damn!" Lego flung himself out of the chair. "I knew it! I knew you'd take this one for yourself. Jeez. How come you always get the good assignments?"

Chase laughed. The kid looked so disappointed, he couldn't help himself. The thing Lego didn't know, and what he wasn't about to tell him, was that he'd already taken Elena for himself, and he'd be damned if he'd let any other guy move in on her. As far as he was concerned, she was already his.

ELENA WAS EXHAUSTED, both physically and mentally. She didn't mind the long work days, so maybe it was a combination of the altitude and heat, but by the time she returned to her CHU each night, she felt completely drained.

The extensive needs of those living on the base floored her, everything from supplying food and laundry services, to heavy drilling equipment and private security guards. The sheer volume of work was overwhelming, but the job was equally satisfying; what she did had an immediate and positive impact on the men and women assigned to the base. Here, there was no time for politics or red tape. The daily needs of the troops were real and urgent, and Elena found it a little daunting to know that she had the ability to authorize or deny those needs with a stroke of her pen.

She and Brad Carrington were the only contracts personnel assigned to the base. Brad had been friendly as he'd briefed Elena on the projects she would oversee, but he'd been all business. Elena was grateful for that, and she sensed that they would work well together. The last thing she needed was another overbearing soldier trying to tell her how to do her job.

After just two days of familiarizing herself with the projects she would be working on, Elena had decided to visit the construction site where a new well was being drilled. She'd heard plenty of horror stories about contracts being awarded for projects that were either unnecessary or bogus. While she doubted that was the case with this project, she wouldn't be satisfied until she saw the ongoing work with her own eyes. Part of her job entailed verifying the progress of the construction, especially since payments were made to the contractor based on the percentage of completion. She was not going to be the contract administrator who authorized millions of dollars for bogus or unnecessary work. When she'd announced her decision to visit the drilling site, Brad had tried to argue that it was unnecessary, but had admitted that he had not seen the project and had little idea how it was progressing.

Elena felt nervous about going out there, but if her job was to oversee the construction projects, then that was what she would do. Brad might roll his eyes and think she was being overly picky, but she sensed that he also had respect for her work ethics. As long as her signature was going on the paperwork to authorize continued performance—and continued payment—she would do everything by the book. At her insistence, Brad had arranged for her to visit the drilling site the following day. She would leave just after dawn and be back on the base by lunchtime.

The sun was setting as she made her way back to her CHU, and she hoped that none of the other women with whom she shared her quarters had yet returned. More than anything, she wanted a few minutes of total quiet. While the female soldiers were respectful to her, Elena felt like an outsider. Actually, she felt like the den mother to a group of rough-and-tumble, foul-mouthed Girl Scouts. The other women could be loud and boisterous, but they were also impossibly young and desperately homesick. They were truck drivers and maintenance technicians, and although technically they weren't in combat positions, they faced the same rigors and dangers that the men did.

Elena wondered how Chase McCormick felt about having them on the base. Just the thought of Chase made her toes curl with longing, even as her teeth clenched in frustration. She'd caught glimpses of him during the past two days and knew he was avoiding her.

Which was fine with her. He occupied her thoughts more than she liked, and the last thing she needed was to get into another confrontation with him. The man was a pigheaded misogynist and she didn't need him distracting her.

"Hey, Ms. De la Vega!"

Elena was just approaching her CHU when the voice interrupted her thoughts, and she turned to see Mike Corrente jogging toward her.

"Hey," she called, genuinely pleased to see him. "When are you going to start calling me Elena?"

He smiled, his teeth white in his dust-covered face. "Maybe when I'm not in uniform and I don't have some badass special ops guy breathing down my neck." He indicated the armful of folders and papers she carried. "Are you done for the day?"

"Yes, just a little nighttime reading. Why?"

"You're moving to new quarters."

"I am?" Elena couldn't keep the surprise from her voice. She knew the housing situation on the base was cramped, at best. Where could they possibly move her to, unless it was into another CHU with a different group of female soldiers?

"Yep. I'll wait here if you want to pack up your gear."

Elena laughed. "I'm not going anywhere, Sergeant. My quarters are fine."

To her surprise, he looked suspiciously smug. "Sorry, but you don't have a choice about it." He glanced at his watch. "I'll give you five minutes, and then I'm coming in to pack up your gear for you."

Her eyebrows shot up at his authoritative tone and he relented. "Trust me on this, okay? You're going to like it."

Elena wasn't so sure she believed him, but she was packed and back outside in just a few minutes, where he hefted her gear over his broad shoulders, leaving her no option but to follow him. He didn't ask about Valerie, although Elena hadn't missed how he stretched his neck to peer inside as she'd opened the door. Not that it would have done any good; the other women were still on patrol through the local villages, performing humanitarian visits.

"So we got a shipment of new CHUs about a week ago, right? And there was a lot of bickering about who was going to get these units, because they're pretty sweet, but there're only six of them. And one of them is yours."

Elena stopped walking. "Mine? As in mine, alone?"

Mike grinned. "Yes, ma'am. C'mon, we're almost there."

He stopped in front of a CHU that looked almost identical to the one she had just vacated, except it was obviously newer. The air-conditioning unit mounted in the wall hummed invitingly, and over the door someone had hung a placard with her last name on it.

Mike opened the door and motioned for her to enter. Elena did so, and stopped just inside the dark, cool interior to stare in amazement. The CHU was the same size as the one she had shared with the other women, but it was designed for just one person. The front part of the unit was a small living area complete with a table and chair and a small desk. Somebody had placed a brightly woven rug on the floor, and tacked a paper sign to the wall that read, "Welcome home, Ms. de la Vega." Standing neatly in a corner was a broom and dustpan.

A crudely constructed wall separated the living area from a tiny bedroom, which held a cot, built-in shelves and a small nightstand. A utilitarian wall lamp had been mounted over the bed for reading.

"What's through here?" Elena asked, indicating a doorway that led to the rear of the unit.

"Go ahead and look," Mike encouraged, dropping her duffel bags onto the cot.

Elena opened the door to a small bathroom. "I get my own shower?" She couldn't keep the amazement out of her voice.

"That's why these units are in such high demand," Mike said. "They're called wet chews, because they come with running water."

Elena turned around to look at Mike in astonishment. "Why do I get one? Surely there are senior military who deserve this more than I do? I'm just a lowly civilian."

Mike shrugged, but Elena didn't miss the color that crept into his cheeks. "We can't have you wandering into the men's showers wearing nothing but a towel. It's, um, distracting."

Elena stared at him for a full minute, until he finally looked away. "How do you know about that?" Her voice was no more than a whisper, and she knew all the color had drained out of her face. Had Chase McCormick said something? She'd been so sure he was above bragging about his conquests. What else did Mike know about that morning?

"Pete Cleary thought he saw your gear inside the changing stall the other morning, and then he saw you come out and go into the women's showers." He glanced at her. "For what it's worth, most of the guys on the base are a decent bunch, but you still have to be careful. Not to mention we have local nationals who work on the base, and if they saw you…" He let his voice trail off meaningfully.

Elena didn't have to guess what he meant. Seeing her come out of the men's showers clad only in a towel would undermine the progress the troops had made in gaining the trust and respect of the local men.

"It was a stupid mistake," she mumbled, brushing a

hand over her eyes. "I was tired, it was dark and I went into the wrong shower. It won't happen again."

"Right. That's why we gave you this unit. So you won't have to worry about making that mistake again."

Was it Elena's imagination, or did Mike refer to something beyond just walking into the wrong shower? Did he know that Chase had been in there with her? Worse, did he know what had happened between them?

Hot color flooded her face, and she couldn't meet his eyes. "Please tell the guys thank you. I love my new digs, and I appreciate the work they did in getting it ready for me."

"Great. I'll let them know." He turned to leave and then paused. "So you're heading out to the drilling site tomorrow, huh?"

Elena nodded. "I want to see the project firsthand and get an estimate on how far they are from completion. It can't hurt for the contractor to know that the project is being closely watched. Not for the kind of money they're getting paid."

"Do you have a firearm?"

"No, of course not. I'm neither trained nor authorized to carry a weapon." Apprehension snaked its way up her spine. "Why? Do you think I'll need one?"

"Who are you traveling with?"

Elena shrugged. "I'm not sure. I was told I'd travel with a security detail."

Mike's mouth tightened. "I'm sure you'll be fine. Just stay close to your men, okay? Don't even go to the bathroom without an escort. Promise?"

"Sure." As if that was going to happen.

But her assurance seemed to placate him, and with a muttered good-night, he left. She watched him leave, plagued with new misgivings about her decision to leave the base. Why would she need a weapon? To protect herself from possible insurgents? Or worse, from the very men who were assigned to protect her?

9

CHASE PAUSED in front of Elena's new housing unit, his hand poised to knock. He could still back out of this detail and give the assignment to Lego. As much as the kid liked to project an air of boyish enthusiasm for everything he did, Chase knew he took his job seriously. He hadn't been exaggerating when he'd said he would take care of Elena.

But while his brain told him that letting Lego handle the assignment was the smart thing to do, every other cell in Chase's body rebelled at the thought. He knew enough about himself to understand that while Elena was away from the base, he'd be unable to concentrate on his own work until she'd returned safely. He and his team were ready to move out, had gone over the covert operation countless times. There wasn't anything more they could do until the operation began.

Blowing out a hard breath, he rapped sharply on Elena's door. The sun had just begun to rise over the horizon, and he wanted to reach the drilling site early. He'd arranged for a convoy of three armored vehicles, each with its own gunner, to travel to the construction site.

He had no reason to expect an attack, but with Elena, he wasn't taking any chances.

He waited a moment and when nobody answered his knock, he rapped again, a little louder. Still nothing. With a muttered curse, he tried the handle, stunned when it turned easily beneath his hand.

"Jesus Christ," he muttered. The woman had absolutely no sense of self-preservation. A dozen different scenarios shot through his mind, each one more unpleasant than the last. Didn't she realize she was on a base with a couple hundred horny, sex-deprived men? While he liked to think none of them would cross that particular line, he'd heard too many horror stories about sexual harassment and rape to think it couldn't happen here.

Opening the door, he stepped quickly inside. A swift glance told him that both the living and sleeping areas were empty. Her bed was neatly made, her combat boots were on the floor and her helmet and flak jacket on a nearby chair. The room smelled of freshly brewed coffee, and he spied a small electric coffeepot on a nearby shelf, with a scant inch of the dark liquid remaining, next to a container of powdered creamer. On the lower shelf were a couple of paperbacks and a framed photo. Curious, he picked it up and studied the faces of Elena and two other women, obviously her sisters. They were almost identical in their dark, sultry beauty. But while one sister was laughing and the other copped a sexy pose for the camera, Elena stared unsmilingly at the lens, almost as if she were afraid to be caught enjoying herself. He placed the frame back on the shelf.

The door beyond the bedroom was closed, but he heard no telltale sound of running water or a flushing toilet. He was getting ready to call her name when the door suddenly opened and there she stood.

In nothing but a pair of black cargo pants and a lacy white bra, and the silver angel charm necklace nestled between her breasts. At the sight of her smooth, bare skin, Chase had to curl his hands at his side to keep from reaching for her.

She came to an abrupt stop when she saw him standing there, and in the instant before she composed her expression, he saw a myriad of emotions flit across her face—surprise, pleasure, apprehension and then embarrassment as she realized she wasn't wearing a shirt. Her face was still damp from where she'd washed it, and now she used the hand towel she'd been holding to cover herself. As if that could keep Chase's imagination from running rampant, recalling in perfect, Technicolor detail just how gorgeous she looked without her bra, her head back, eyes heavy-lidded and lips parted as he suckled her.

"Don't you knock?" she asked sharply, pushing past him to snatch a folded jersey from the shelf beside her bed.

Chase kept his back turned as she thrust her arms through the sleeves and dragged it over head.

"You should lock your door," he said over his shoulder. "Just because you're on an American base doesn't mean you're safe."

She snorted. "Obviously."

He did turn around then, both relieved and disappointed to see she was decently covered. She sat on the edge of the bed and bent over to pull her boots on. Every inch of her bristled with resentment. He knew exactly why she was pissed off. Chase didn't blame her for being angry with him, but he couldn't feel bad about ending their encounter in the shower.

If anyone had come in…

He told himself again that he'd done them both a favor by pushing her away. She'd never know how difficult that had been for him.

"So you're going out to the drilling site today."

She glanced up at him, her hair spilling over her shoulder in sleek, dark waves. "That's right, and don't even think about trying to talk me out of it. I have a job to do, and visiting the project sites is part of it. I have a military escort, so I'll be just fine."

She stood up and he watched, mesmerized, as she swept her hair back and secured it with a ponytail holder she'd had around her wrist. The DPA uniform should have given her an androgynous appearance, but the tan, cotton T-shirt only emphasized the feminine swell of her breasts, and she filled out the seat of her cargo pants in a way that could never be mistaken for a man. Even without makeup and with her stony expression, she was prettier than she had a right to be.

"I know you'll be fine," he replied smoothly.

Pointedly ignoring him, Elena grabbed her DPA cap from a nearby hook and jammed it onto her head, dragging her ponytail through the opening at the back. Picking up her helmet and vest she finally turned to Chase.

"If you don't mind, my ride leaves in a few minutes. I have to get going."

Chase nodded, keeping his expression bland. "Absolutely. That's why I'm here. Let's go." He indicated she should precede him out of the trailer, but she just stood there and stared at him. He knew the precise instant when she realized the truth.

"Oh, no," she said, laughing in disbelief. "You are so not coming with me."

Chase crossed his arms over his chest and gave her what he hoped was a bland smile. "Fine. Then you don't go."

"You don't even like me," she spluttered. "Why would you want to spend an entire morning with me?"

Didn't like her? Was that really what she thought? Didn't she realize that his problem had to do with liking her way too much? He wanted to peel her uniform from her body, lower her to the small cot and spend the entire day worshipping her with his hands and mouth. Since she'd shown up, he'd hardly slept, could barely focus on his own job and was swiftly becoming a joke among his own men. And she thought he didn't *like* her?

"Look," he said, striving for a reasonable tone, "I think we got off on a wrong foot somewhere." Like when she'd wanted to go down on him and he had pushed her away. Yeah, way to convince her that you really like her.

She watched him warily, and he blew out a hard breath. "I know we jumped the gun back in Kuwait, and it might seem like there's no place for our relationship to go from here, but…"

"But what?"

He hesitated. He desperately wanted to get to know Elena better. Hell, he wanted nothing more than to make love to her, right here and now. He wanted two uninterrupted weeks with her in this room. But he also knew Afghanistan was no place for a budding romance, and that he had no business encouraging her to have feelings for him. Soon enough, she'd return to the States while he'd still be here. And how difficult would that be? Not just for him, but for her, too.

He'd been thirteen when his father had left for the first Gulf War, and he'd seen the toll that his absence had taken on his mother. She'd tried to be strong for Chase and his sisters, but she hadn't fooled him. She'd gone through hell, not knowing if her husband was safe. Chase didn't want to put a woman through that uncertainty. Did he want to settle down and have kids? Sure. But not now. Not when he spent more time deployed than he did at home. But he'd be lying if he said he didn't want a relationship with Elena. Maybe, when his deployment was up…if she was still interested…

"Look, I'd like to get to know you, and I want you to get to know me, too." He laughed softly and pinched the bridge of his nose. "I don't blame you if you're not interested, because I've been kinda hard on you, but you have to believe that I meant it in the best possible way."

She narrowed her eyes at him, one hand on her hip. "What is it, *exactly,* that you want from me, Chase? You've been giving me mixed signals since I showed up, and I'd really like to know. Do you want to pick up where we left off? Or would you rather just pretend I don't exist? Because either way, I really don't care. It's your call. Just let me know so I don't end up making an idiot of myself, okay?"

Either way, I really don't care. He knew she was lying, giving him a show of bravado to hide the fact that she did care. Every fiber of his being wanted to shout, *Yes, let's pick up exactly where we left off, with you getting ready to make me go blind with pleasure.* Instead, he forced himself to smile at her in what he hoped was a platonic way.

"I think we could be friends," he finally said, knowing he was lying through his teeth and hating himself for it. The way he felt about Elena went way past friendship. A true friend wouldn't think about licking every inch of her skin, or about how she looked straddling his thighs as he thrust into her.

He watched as her mouth opened and then snapped shut. She stared at him as if he'd suddenly sprouted a third eye in the middle of his forehead.

"Friends." She repeated the word in disbelief, but her hazel eyes began to shimmer hotly. "You want to be *friends?*"

"Yeah."

"I see."

But he knew that she didn't.

She thought that he didn't want her, that he wasn't interested in her that way. The truth was, he wanted to possess her, to claim her as his own so that she would know it, and so would everyone else on the base. But he also knew that going public with their relationship would be a huge mistake. It was tough enough to be a female in a military environment without the added label of being an easy screw, and warranted or not, he knew that's how the soldiers would view her. He was doing her a huge favor by keeping their relationship platonic. And if that pissed her off, too bad. At least the other guys wouldn't bother her.

"Fine," she muttered, giving him a tight little smile. "Let's be *friends.*"

"Great." He forced a smile. "Now put on your helmet and vest."

"But we're not even off the base yet," she protested.

"Just put them on," he commanded, and watched as she struggled into the heavy gear.

"So what did you do to end up having to accompany me out to the drilling site?" she asked, glancing sideways at him and then away. "Forget it. I can see by your face that there was never going to be anyone but you."

And there never will be.

Whoa! Chase had no idea where that thought had come from. He had no room in his life for a permanent relationship, and he certainly didn't intend to tie himself down to a prickly, argumentative woman like Elena de la Vega. The woman was too hot-blooded. Too hot, period.

They made their way to the motor pool as the sun began to rise over the distant mountains. The air was still cool, but Chase knew that in a matter of hours the temperatures would climb back into the nineties and higher. He could hear the throaty, diesel rumbling of the engines before they actually reached the three heavily armored trucks, called MRAPs, that were lined up, ready to go. Chase nodded to the gunners who sat in round turrets on top of each vehicle, manning a 50-caliber machine gun. Small groups of soldiers stood talking, each dressed in full combat gear.

Elena stopped and Chase could see she looked a little stunned. "I thought we'd simply go in a single Humvee," she said, staring at the convoy of armored trucks. "Do we really need all these men?"

"We're in a war environment," Chase reminded her. "Each time we leave the base we need to be prepared for an attack. These vehicles are specifically designed to withstand that."

When she turned to look at him, he could see her face had paled and her eyes were huge in her face. She swallowed hard. Any second now, she'd change her mind and cancel the trip. He could see her weighing the options and calculating the risks. He knew exactly what she was thinking. So many men, so many resources being dedicated to her, just so that she could visit a construction site and verify that work was progressing to her satisfaction.

He knew that only a few of her predecessors had ever gone out to visit the project sites. Not even the chicken-shit Lieutenant Commander Carrington made any effort to visit the construction sites, preferring to remain within the perimeter of the base. Like most of the contract administrators who'd been here before him, he simply took the contractors' word that the projects were being done in accordance with the terms of the contracts and paid them accordingly. Which was partially why the government was losing its financial shirt to dishonest contractors, and paying for work that was either shoddy, incomplete or unnecessary.

She drew a deep breath. "Which vehicle do I ride in?"

He shouldn't be surprised that she was going to go through with it. Elena struck him as a woman who, once she made up her mind about something, followed through on it.

"The second one," he answered, and indicated she should climb inside. He followed close behind her. There was no way he was letting her out of his sight.

ELENA CLIMBED into the vehicle, glad that she didn't suffer from claustrophobia. The interior was relatively spacious, with two benches that hung along each wall, facing each other, but it felt a little like a sardine can. Behind the driver's seat was a tall platform for the gunner, who sat in a leather sling seat with his upper body protruding through a hole in the ceiling as he manned the turret gun.

Elena took a seat against one wall and noted the extensive digital electronics built into the interior. The vehicle was like something she'd imagine seeing in a futuristic sci-fi movie. Chase climbed in behind her and then pushed a button, raising and closing the pneumatic rear doors and sealing them into the small space.

"This is, um, pretty impressive," she finally said.

Chase sat down across from her, laying his weapon over his thighs. His knees almost touched hers. "You bet. These vehicles are designed to withstand a direct hit from an IED—an improvised explosive device. The hull is V-shaped to deflect the blast outward."

"Have there been many, uh, attacks in this region?"

His face softened fractionally, and Elena wondered if he could see her fear. "There've been a couple of attacks, but none recently."

Something in his expression said he wasn't being completely truthful, but she also instinctively knew that he'd never allow her to visit the drilling site if he thought she might be in danger.

"How long will it take to get there?"

"Not long. The site is just outside a small village about two miles from here. The road is pretty rough, which will slow us down a bit, but we should be there in under twenty minutes."

"I read that the villagers will also benefit from the well."

"That's right. Part of our mission is to win the hearts and minds of the local people, so anything we can do to improve their situation only benefits us."

The driver and a second soldier climbed into the cab of the truck, and looked back at Elena and Chase. "Everyone comfortable?"

"You bet," Chase answered. He looked over at Elena. "Hold on to something. The road gets a little bumpy."

He wasn't kidding. The loudness of the engines, combined with the swaying and tipping of the vehicle as it traversed the road, made conversation nearly impossible. Above her, the gunner rocked in his sling seat, his booted feet planted firmly on the platform as he surveyed their surroundings. Elena found her initial apprehension fading, and she felt a sense of excitement at being embedded as part of a military convoy.

All too soon, the vehicle began to slow, and Chase rose to his feet to lean through the opening into the driver's cab. He spoke in low tones and Elena couldn't make out what was being said.

"We're here," he announced unnecessarily as they came to a stop. He lowered the rear door, and Elena blinked at the sudden brightness.

She climbed out of the MRAP and realized they had driven onto what looked like a military compound, complete with razor-wire fencing, guards and temporary buildings. But dominating the small complex was a large, steel drilling machine, and its rhythmic pounding shook the ground and reverberated through her body. Stacked on the ground beside the drill were a dozen or more lengths of wide pipe, each nearly thirty feet in length. As she watched, two men in military uniform carefully inserted a pipe into the mechanism.

"What are they doing?" she asked.

"Drilling," Chase answered sardonically. "C'mon, I'll introduce you to the project manager." He glanced at his watch. "You have two hours to conduct your business, and then we're leaving."

The time passed swiftly for Elena. She and the project manager, a civilian contractor named Bill, took a tour of the compound and he explained the mechanics of drilling for water. Inside his trailer, they reviewed progress reports and charts, and Elena learned that pipe was being laid from the well site to both the forward operating base and to the nearby village. Even when the well was completed, they would need to maintain a security detail at the site to prevent insurgents from destroying it. But having a water source would enable the troops to be more independent and provide the villagers with a clean water source that they didn't need to pay for.

During the entire visit, Elena was all too aware of the big soldier who dogged her footsteps. Chase never let her out of his sight, taking his role as her personal bodyguard seriously. He didn't participate in her conversations with the workers, or indicate that he was at all interested in the papers that she pored over or that he even understood them, but she sensed that he missed nothing. All too soon, he indicated that their time at the site was up. She might have protested, but the implacable expression on his face said he wouldn't change his mind on this. Reluctantly, Elena said goodbye to the construction team and climbed back inside the MRAP.

"That was amazing," she said to Chase. "I have a whole new appreciation for the work being done over here. I wish my coworkers back home could see this."

The thought reminded her of Larry, who had scoffed

when she'd told him that she'd be deploying to Afghanistan. What would he think if he could see her now? In the next instant, she realized she didn't really care. Her relationship with Larry might have occurred in another lifetime. Even the thought of him with that other woman didn't cause her chest to tighten.

Sitting across from Chase, with his rock-hard body and unflappable attitude, she couldn't imagine what she'd ever found attractive about Larry. Chase was the most unapologetically masculine guy she'd ever met, but she also knew he had a softer side that he allowed few people to see.

Back in Kuwait, he'd been so honest with her about not wanting to lead her on. She'd even called him sweet. He hadn't appreciated her description, but she knew it was true. He could be both lethal and incredibly tender, and she found the combination completely irresistible. She knew he wanted her. She'd caught him watching her several times during the trip, when he didn't think she'd notice. The heat she'd seen in his eyes had brought her right back to the shower incident, and she'd had to press her thighs tightly together and try to ignore the sharp stab of arousal she'd felt.

He'd made it clear that he didn't want her in Afghanistan, but since she'd arrived at the forward operating base, she'd realized that she was a lot tougher than she gave herself credit for. Now she just had to convince Chase of that.

"You're smiling," he observed, watching her.

"Am I?"

His eyes narrowed fractionally. "What's going through that head of yours?"

But she just shook her head. "Nothing. Really."

She could see he didn't believe her, but she wasn't about to reveal her thoughts to him. Six months ago, she'd never have considered working in Afghanistan, or traveling to a construction site with an armed military escort. There were so many things she would never have considered doing six months ago, and having a one-night stand with a guy like Chase McCormick topped the list.

But she'd done all those things and more. She'd surprised herself with her own capabilities. She knew Chase didn't want her on the base, but she had to believe that she'd impressed him today, just a little bit, with her abilities. Now she was going to take it one step further.

He'd said he wanted to be friends, but Elena knew from the way he looked at her that he wanted more than just *friendship*. Six months ago—six days ago—she might not have had the courage to take a risk and go after what she really wanted. But not anymore. And she really wanted Chase McCormick.

She was going to show him that she could be effective, both on the base and in the bedroom.

His bedroom, to be precise.

10

IT HAD BEEN A MISTAKE to accompany Elena to the drilling site. He'd been okay as long as he'd been able to think of her in terms of a woman he'd like to nail, versus a woman he had to respect. Chase wasn't proud of himself for his Neanderthal attitude, but it was a hell of a lot easier to maintain an emotional distance when he told himself that she was just a pretty face without too much else going on.

But the morning's visit to the drilling site had shattered that illusion. The fact was, Elena de la Vega was both beautiful *and* brilliant. He'd pretty much glued himself to her side during the visit, ready to either whisk her to the safety of the MRAP or protect her with his own body if the need had arisen. Which, thank Christ, it hadn't.

But the downside of eavesdropping on her professional discussions was that he could no longer fool himself. She'd asked pointed questions of the project manager and the engineers and had been able to decipher their spreadsheets and charts within minutes. She'd pointed out inconsistencies, made recommendations

for improvements and—much to his disappointment—
had promised to return to the site to check on the
progress.

But even more disturbing than her keen mind…she'd
been personable and charming. She'd smiled and laughed
with the men, and he'd known the instant that they'd
each fallen under her spell, spilling their guts about the
problems they were encountering, and even going so far
as to admit that some of their invoiced costs were exces-
sive. Through it all, she'd smiled and nodded and taken
notes, and none of them had seemed to understand that
she wasn't their friend. She had all the control, and she
could tighten the purse strings to their accounts until
they choked.

He'd tried to see her through their eyes and acknowledged that she must be like a tall, cool drink of water
after enduring the dust and heat and threat of death for
months on end. Even wearing a helmet and flak vest
over her DPA uniform, she didn't resemble a soldier. She
could have been a visiting dignitary or a celebrity on a
USO tour, here to cheer up the troops. She'd certainly
cheered up the guys at the construction site. At one point,
the project manager had placed a hand at the small of
her back to guide her into his work trailer. Even knowing
that Elena couldn't have been aware of his hand through
her flak vest, Chase had wanted to pick the man up and
throw him across the threshold.

Now he watched her as she sat across from him, a
small smile lifting the corners of her gorgeous mouth.
He couldn't stop thinking about how her lips had felt
against his own. Soft and lush. And when those lips had
moved lower, across his torso and over his abdomen…
oh, man.

He realized he was getting turned on and adjusted his rifle across his thighs to hide the evidence. In the same instant, he realized she was talking to him and he hadn't heard a word she said.

"Huh?" Oh, that was good. Way to impress the lady. He regrouped. "Sorry, I was thinking about something else and missed what you said. Repeat?"

Her smile widened, as if she knew exactly what he'd been thinking. "I asked if it's okay to take my helmet off, seeing as we're in an armored truck. I'm so hot, and my head itches."

"Sure, just hold on to something while we're moving." He indicated the low ceiling. He was back in control. "We've had guys whack their heads while going over rough ground."

Reaching up, she unsnapped her helmet and removed it, and placed it on the floor between her feet. Chase couldn't look away as she pulled her hair free from the ponytail holder and shook it out, then worked her fingers into the glossy strands to massage her scalp. She gave a blissful sigh and tipped her head back against the wall. Her eyes drifted closed.

Chase curled his hands onto his thighs. Even from where he sat, he could smell her shampoo, and his fingers itched to wrap themselves in her hair. He admired the slender column of her throat and the delicate line of her jaw, remembering how soft her skin had been beneath his fingertips. Beneath his lips.

And just like that, he was hard again.

"Hey, Sergeant!"

Chase jumped guiltily and leaned forward to look at the soldier sitting in the front passenger seat. "What is it, Corporal?"

"Looks like market day in the village. Wanna stop?"

Elena had opened her eyes and was sitting upright, straining to catch a glimpse of the village through the windshield. Her gaze swung toward Chase, and he already knew what she was going to ask.

"Can we do that? Is it safe?"

Chase hesitated. Normally, they would stop the vehicles and greet the villagers. They would exchange courtesies with the elders, pass out candy to the kids, purchase goods from the market stands, all part of their campaign toward winning the loyalty of the local population. But today he had to think about Elena. The responsibility of keeping her safe was a huge weight on his shoulders.

"Sergeant?" asked the corporal. "The lead truck wants to know if we stop or keep moving."

Chase made the mistake of glancing at Elena. He saw the excitement and hope in her eyes and knew he couldn't say no.

"We'll stop," he replied gruffly. "Twenty minutes, max."

Elena gave him a beautiful smile, and Chase felt something shift in his chest. "Thank you," she said.

Instead of acknowledging her thanks, he reached into a pocket and pulled out a camouflage bandana. He always kept several handy in case of sandstorms, and now he shoved it unceremoniously at Elena.

"Here, cover your head."

She took the cloth and stared at him, then shook it out and began to arrange it over her hair. Chase watched her struggle with it for several seconds before he made a sound of impatience. Setting his weapon on the bench, he crouched in front of her.

"Not like that," he admonished softly. "You need to cover your hair and your neck."

Taking the bandana from her, he shook it out and refolded it, and then draped it over her head. She was so close that he could feel the warmth of her breath against his face, and see the tiny pulse that beat frantically at the base of her smooth throat.

He swallowed hard, forcing himself to concentrate on his task. "Take the ends, like this," he said, "and bring them around the front. Then cross them at the throat and tie them like so, behind your neck."

He had to reach behind her to secure the ends of the cloth, and he didn't miss how her breathing hitched. He forced his hands to remain steady as he tied a knot and then rocked back on his heels to survey his handiwork. She looked like a beautiful peasant girl, or give her a pair of big, dark sunglasses and she'd look like a Hollywood movie star. Her cheeks were flushed and her eyes were focused on him with such intensity that his pulse tripped into overdrive.

"Here," he muttered, "your hair is still sticking out." He raised a hand to push the escaped strands beneath the cloth, then froze when she turned her cheek into his palm.

"Chase," she murmured, her gaze drifting over his face to settle on his mouth.

Jesus. He was going to kiss her; he couldn't stop himself. Nothing short of a direct rocket attack would prevent him from covering her mouth with his own, right there in the back of the MRAP, with two junior soldiers sitting just feet away.

He bent his head toward her. Her lips parted, but at the last second she pulled away and ducked beneath his arm to snatch her helmet from the floor. In the same instant, the pneumatic door at the back of the truck lifted open and two soldiers peered inside.

Chase sat on his heels for a moment, head down, fighting for composure. He'd come so close to losing it.

"Hey, Sarge, you okay?" asked one of the men.

"Yeah." Reaching out, he snatched his weapon from the bench and jumped down from the back of the vehicle before turning to assist Elena. But she had already taken the corporal's proffered hand, and he was leading her to the little village where children ran toward them in anticipation.

He watched as she bent down to greet the children, and within seconds she was surrounded by a sea of tiny arms, reaching up toward her.

"I gave her a box of candy," the corporal explained with a self-satisfied grin. "The universal icebreaker."

"Twenty minutes," Chase said gruffly, "and then I want her back in this truck."

As much as he wanted to be within arm's reach of Elena, he stood back a dozen or so paces. He didn't trust himself to get any closer. He followed her as the children took her hands and dragged her over to a tiny marketplace to show her the colorful array of handwoven scarves and tassels, tiny bells that hung from embroidered loops and strings of beads carved from stone. He knew he should back off and let a couple of the junior officers watch over her. He should be greeting the village elders and making nice with the tribal leader, but right now all he wanted was to watch Elena.

She lingered over a selection of hand-knotted rugs, and two local women, heavily draped in mustard-yellow cloth, shyly offered her a cup of Chai tea. She looked toward Chase for permission, and he gave her a barely perceptible shake of his head. He didn't want to be rude, but the drawn-out ritual of drinking tea would take longer than he planned for them to be there.

He watched as she pulled a wallet out of her cargo pants and began bargaining with the women, and even from a distance he could hear their soft voices and musical laughter. The children laughed, too, and Chase groaned. Great. Even with the language and cultural barriers, she did a better job of winning hearts and minds than his men did.

"Hey, Sergeant," called one of the soldiers, "we should get going. Looks like a storm's brewing in the east."

Chase looked to the horizon, where an ominous reddish cloud had formed, darkening the sky. A dust storm, by the looks of it. He knew from experience the damage that blowing sand and grit could do to an engine. No way would he risk breaking down out here. Neither would he let their convoy be overtaken by the looming cloud, which could reduce visibility to zero. They needed to get back to the base ASAP, and batten down the hatches.

"Elena," he finally called, "we need to go."

She nodded to the women, hugged several of the children and turned back to him, her arms spilling over with bright textiles and shiny beads.

"Look at all this," she exclaimed as she reached him. She was breathless with excitement. "These people made these beautiful things with their own hands."

"How much did you give them?"

Elena laughed. "I have no idea, but I don't care. It was worth every penny."

"Leave it to a woman to find a shopping opportunity, even in the middle of nowhere," he said wryly, but he couldn't help smiling at her enthusiasm.

Chase didn't relax until they were back inside the MRAP and rumbling along the road toward the base. Elena spread her purchases out on the bench beside her. He thought she would show each item to him, and found he was actually looking forward to seeing what she had bought. Instead, she smoothed a hand almost reverently over an embroidered shawl and grew quiet.

"What's wrong?" he asked. "I thought you enjoyed your shopping adventure."

He was teasing her, hoping to elicit another laugh. God, he loved to hear her laugh. But when she looked up, he saw a deep sadness in her eyes.

"I did enjoy it," she murmured, "but at the same time it made me so sad."

"Because you've suddenly realized that your wallet is empty?" he teased.

She gave him a half smile. "No. It's just that beauty like this should be shared and seen by many people, not just those stationed in Afghanistan. The people are so gracious and lovely." She gave a deep sigh. "Someday, I'd like to come back here as a tourist. When the country is safe, and I can visit these villages without an armed escort and accept an invitation to have tea."

Ah, man. Not just beautiful and brilliant, but sensitive and caring, too.

"Someday," he said softly, wishing it could come true. For her.

THE MRAP SHUDDERED to a stop. Chase was on his feet in an instant, peering through the windshield to see the reason.

"What is it?" he asked the driver.

"Looks like an accident up ahead, Sarge," the driver replied. "Ah, shit, that looks like one of our vehicles."

Elena stood up, peering over Chase's shoulders, but she couldn't see past the lead MRAP.

Chase hit the pneumatic doors and grabbed his weapon, preparing to jump down from the vehicle. He turned at the last minute and pointed a finger at Elena, and his voice was deadly serious.

"You. Stay. Here. Until we know whether this is an accident or something more, you're not to leave this vehicle, understood?"

She nodded, and watched as he sprinted toward the front of the convoy. She peered up at the gunner who was surveying the entire scene from his perch on top of the MRAP.

"Can you see what's going on?" she shouted up to him.

"Looks like an accident with a Humvee and a jingle truck."

"Is anyone hurt?"

"I can't tell, ma'am," he called down to her. "Wait! I see a kid! There was a kid in the truck and it looks like he's been injured."

Which meant this was an accident, not an ambush. At that instant, the radio in the cab squawked and she heard Chase's voice.

"Charlie Company, we need a medic ASAP. We have a child, possible broken bones and lacerations. Over."

"Roger that," replied the soldier sitting in the passenger's seat. Reaching down, he pulled a medical kit from beneath his seat and leaped from the vehicle.

Elena didn't wait to see more. She climbed down from the MRAP and ran toward the front of the convoy. A Humvee that had been driving in the opposite direction lay on its side in a ditch beside the road. The brightly decorated jingle truck, so called for the assortment of chains and pendants that swung from the front bumper, rested nose down in a ditch on the other side of the road.

Soldiers from both the Humvee and the MRAPs swarmed the area, assessing the damage and standing guard in case this was more than just an accident. Two of the soldiers carried a young boy from the truck and laid him carefully on the road. A man followed, dressed in a long white shirt and baggy pants, his head wrapped in a turban, his face creased in worry. The boy's father, Elena thought. She could see the boy's face was covered with blood.

Chase and another soldier bent over the child, speaking to him in soothing tones as they assessed his injuries. Elena crouched beside Chase, ignoring the dark look he angled at her. The boy was conscious, and she could see fear in his huge, dark eyes. Nearby, the father spoke rapidly to one of the soldiers, gesturing with his hands.

"Is he going to be okay?" Elena asked quietly, looking at the little boy. God, he was just a baby.

"I thought I told you to stay in the truck," Chase said between gritted teeth.

Elena watched as his hands moved with gentle skill over the child, checking for broken bones and internal injuries. She blew out a hard breath. "I couldn't stay in there and not know what was happening out here. How is he?"

Chase took the boy's arm in his big hands and deftly probed his wrist, which hung at an awkward angle. The child gave a sharp cry. "Broken wrist, and he'll need stitches for the head wound."

"Shouldn't he go to a hospital?" she asked.

"He should absolutely go to a hospital," Chase agreed grimly, "but there isn't one for several hundred miles. Fortunately, his injuries aren't life-threatening. We'll take him back to the base and patch him up there."

"Sir, I'm going to splint the wrist and put a bandage on the laceration," the medic said, but as soon as he tried to swab the child's head, the boy began thrashing in panic.

Without thinking, Elena moved to the boy, lifting his head and settling it on her lap. She stroked his hair, careful not to touch the nasty gash on his forehead.

"Tell him that everything's going to be okay," she said, speaking to Chase.

He stared at her for an instant, and then repeated the words to the child in a language that Elena had never heard before. The child stopped struggling, but still cried.

"Tell him he's a very brave boy, and he's going to have something to brag about to the other boys when he gets home." She listened as Chase translated for her. He must have added something else, because he grinned and winked at the child, and earned a quick laugh in return.

The medic swabbed the wound and quickly applied a bandage. "That will do until we get back to the base," he said, "but I still want to splint the wrist."

The boy cried out when the medic lifted his arm, and Chase held him down with one hand on the child's narrow chest to keep him from struggling. Reaching behind her neck, Elena unfastened her necklace and dangled the angel charm where the boy could see it.

"Tell him that this angel will keep him safe, and that there is nothing to be afraid of."

The child quieted as Chase repeated her words, his eyes fastened on the sparkling necklace. Elena continued to speak to the boy, soothing him until the medic finished fastening the splint.

"All set," he said. "No pun intended. We should move him to the MRAP and get him to the base."

While Chase went to coordinate uprighting the overturned Humvee and getting the jingle truck back on the road, Elena stayed with the child. He had pushed himself into a sitting position on the dusty road, and his father crouched beside him, talking gently to him and patting him on the head.

"Here," Elena said, fastening the necklace around the boy's neck. "I want you to have this. That way, you'll always have someone to watch over you and keep you safe."

She looked up as Chase translated her words to the child. She had thought he was out of hearing range. The boy looked down at the little angel around his neck and then at Elena, and said something to Chase.

"He wants to know your name," Chase interpreted.

Elena told him, and watched as the boy repeated her name several times. He pointed to himself. "Kadir," he said proudly.

"Kadir," Elena repeated. "It was a pleasure to meet you."

Kadir looked up at Chase and asked a question, and Chase solemnly replied in the boy's language. Kadir looked satisfied and didn't object as Chase lifted him up and carried him to the waiting MRAP.

Elena watched as he settled the boy inside and then helped the father climb in beside the child. When the door had closed, he banged on the side of the vehicle.

"Let's move out," he called. He turned to the soldiers who struggled to get the two vehicles back onto the road. "Step it up, boys! This storm isn't going to wait for us."

When they were back in the MRAP and moving again, Elena looked at Chase. "You were very good with the child. Are you a medic?"

"It's not my specialty, but I have field training. Any of the others could have treated him just as easily." His beautiful mouth lifted at one corner. "He was pretty taken with you. Another conquest, it seems."

Elena felt her cheeks warm beneath his regard. "I only did what his mother would have done. But you did a great job." She hesitated. "What did he ask you, just before you picked him up?"

He didn't pretend to misunderstand. "You gave him your guardian angel. He wanted to know who would watch over you and keep *you* safe."

"What did you say?" Her voice was breathless.

Chase's eyes glittered hotly. "I told him that's my job."

11

BY THE TIME they reached the base, the wind had kicked up, and great eddies of dust swirled around the low buildings. While the medics brought Kadir and his father to the base clinic, Chase walked Elena to her quarters but declined her invitation for a cup of coffee. Realistically, Elena knew he couldn't come in. Even if it wasn't the middle of a workday, there were rules against being alone with the opposite sex in your private quarters, and Chase had made it clear that he supported those rules. Leaving her door open for propriety's sake wasn't an option, either. Not with the crap that was blowing around outside.

"Thanks for coming with me today," she said, standing inside her doorway.

"No problem." His voice was brusque. Professional. "Listen, this storm is just going to get worse. If we lose power, don't panic. The generators will kick on and the lights will come right back up. Do you have a supply of water in your hut?"

"Not a supply, no. Just a couple of bottles that I use to make coffee with. I haven't really had a chance to stock up on anything. Except coffee." She laughed a little. "I have an addiction to the stuff."

Chase had removed his helmet and now he scrubbed a hand over his short hair. "Okay, I'll ask one of the guys to bring a case over to you. What about food? Do you have anything to eat inside?"

Elena shook her head again. "Nope. Nothing. But don't worry about me, Chase. You're not responsible for me. I can always walk over to the chow hall. It's not that far. Anyway, I should probably head over to my office to see if Brad needs a hand."

She watched his beautiful mouth tighten, but didn't know if it was due to her use of the lieutenant's first name, or out of concern for her safety.

"Absolutely not. Once this thing hits, we're going to lose daylight. Only essential emergency personnel will be permitted outdoors. You're better off remaining in your quarters. I'm going over to the chow hall myself. What can I bring back for you?"

Elena leaned against the door frame and considered him. Something had changed about Chase. She wouldn't exactly describe him as *softer,* but he was definitely more approachable than he had been just days earlier. More like the man she had known in Kuwait. More like the man who had completely rocked her world and then tucked a note inside her duffel bag that said he wasn't ready to say goodbye.

"Aren't you violating your own rules?" she asked softly. "I mean, this is beginning to sound an awful lot like preferential treatment, if you ask me."

To his credit, his expression didn't change. "Not at all," he said smoothly. "It's actually safer for me to bring something back to you than to have you get lost out here until the dust settles. Literally. Besides, you can't carry a case of water, and the DPA would have my ass if I let you starve to death in your trailer."

Elena smiled, not at all fooled. Whether Chase acknowledged it to himself or not, there was a part of him that wanted to protect her.

They had a connection.

"Okay, thanks," she said, relenting. "I'll just have whatever you're having."

He grinned then, his teeth a flash of white in his handsome face, and Elena recalled again why she had fallen so easily into bed with him. The guy was walking sex in combat boots. She watched as he jogged back the way they had come, and then closed the door.

The storm hadn't yet reached them and already there was sand everywhere. A fine coating had settled on every surface, and Elena spent the next thirty minutes wiping down the tables and shelves, shaking out her bedding, and sweeping the floor. Not that it really made a difference; the stuff was insidious, finding its way through the chinks in the doors and windows.

Once she had removed the worst of the dust, she used her new purchases to transform the stark interior of the trailer, draping an embroidered shawl over the table and covering the floor with brightly woven rugs. She hung another shawl on the wall in the living area, and used three more to create a hanging curtain around her bed, tying them back with the hand-knotted tassels.

When she was finished, she stood back to admire her handiwork. Nothing could really disguise the fact that she was living in a prefab trailer, and there was no way that the plywood and two-by-four construction could be described as cozy, but the addition of the fabrics was definitely an improvement. But now she felt grimy and uncomfortable. Glancing at her watch, she saw that nearly an hour had passed since Chase had left. Until the well was operational, even bath water was rationed and she didn't have enough water remaining in her storage tank for a nice, hot shower. Maybe a quick sponge bath, though.

There was a brief knock at her door, and then it just about blew open, bringing in a whole new load of sand and dust. Elena's eyes widened as both Pete Cleary and Mike Corrente stumbled inside. Mike kicked the door shut with one booted foot and then turned around, grunting under the weight of two cases of bottled water.

"Where do you want these, ma'am?" he asked. He wore a pair of clear goggles and his face was covered in grit, turning his eyebrows into fuzzy caterpillars. Without waiting for a reply, he set both cases of water down on her little table. "This should keep you for a while."

Pete carried two large brown bags in his arms, sealed at the top. He set them down next to the water and pushed his own goggles to the top of his head. Only the skin around his eyes was free of the red dust, giving him a distinct raccoon appearance. "McCormick sent this over," he explained. "Enough food to keep you going for a couple of days, at least."

The fact that he'd sent two soldiers to bring her supplies wasn't lost on Elena. He was still looking out for her reputation. But holy moley, she was just one person. Did she really need two cases of water and what looked like enough food to feed an army? Did that mean he wasn't planning on seeing her for a good, long time? That he intended for her to ride out the storm by herself?

"Where is Sergeant McCormick?" she asked.

Pete shrugged. "I couldn't say. He just asked us to make sure you had enough supplies to make it through the storm."

Mike was looking around the small living area, and now he whistled through his teeth. "I like what you've done with the place. Very homey. Very nice."

"Thanks." Elena hugged her arms around her middle and tried not to let her disappointment show. Why should it matter who brought her supplies? Realistically she knew that Chase had more important things to do than play delivery boy.

"Yep, I think it's safe to say that McCormick wouldn't have done nearly as nice a job decorating this place as you've done," observed Pete.

Elena stared at him. What was he saying? That the CHU she was living in had originally been meant for Chase?

"Nice job, asshole," muttered Mike.

Pete frowned and made a pretense of cleaning his goggles.

"Wait," Elena said. "Are you telling me that this is Chase's trailer?"

"Well, he never actually lived in it. We got a shipment of CHUs for the special ops guys, but Chase said he didn't want one. He said he didn't need all this space," explained Pete.

"So where does he sleep?"

"He bunks with a couple of his team members."

Elena digested this bit of information. Chase had opted to give *her* the unit that had been meant for him. Preferential treatment, indeed.

She was also sure that he hadn't wanted her to find out

about his grand sacrifice. Because then he'd be revealed as a complete hypocrite. A softy.

"Listen," began Mike, "I'm pretty sure he didn't want you to know…"

"I won't say anything to him," she assured the two men who stood in her living area, looking apprehensive.

Pete gave a huff of laughter. "Thanks. He'd have my ass if he knew I told you. Hey, if you, uh, want some company until this thing blows over, I'd be happy to stay with you. These storms can pass in a matter of hours, or they can sometimes last for days." He shifted his weight, but Elena didn't miss the hopeful look on his face.

"Oh, well, that's very considerate of you," she began.

"You bet."

"But completely unnecessary," she finished. "You see, I have, um, some paperwork to complete from the site visit today, and it will probably take me a while to finish. I won't even notice the storm."

"Maybe we should both stay," Mike countered, shooting a dark look in Pete's direction.

Elena laughed. "I'm pretty sure there are rules against that, and you probably both have a ton of work to do. I'll be fine." They looked doubtful, and Elena felt a flash of irritation. Did she really come across as being that helpless? "*Really.* I'll be fine," she said more firmly. "Now go."

They did, but only reluctantly. Elena closed the door behind them and locked it, grateful to be alone. The knowledge that Chase had given her his housing unit still stunned her. What had prompted him to do such a thing?

She unpacked the food he had sent over, smiling at

the selection Chase had provided. He'd sent bread and
fruit and a dozen snack packages of cheese and crackers.
There were chocolate-pudding packs, and granola bars.
And at the bottom of the bag, wrapped in wax paper, a
thick turkey sandwich which she devoured, washing it
down with a bottle of water.

She hadn't been lying when she'd told Pete and Mike
that she had paperwork to do from her visit to the drilling site, and after stacking her food supplies neatly on
the shelf, she sat down at her desk and began to work. It
seemed only an hour had passed when she heard what
sounded like a police radio.

Standing up, she pushed back the curtain on the window and peered outside. A Humvee made its way slowly
through the housing area, and a voice spoke through a
loudspeaker.

"Seek shelter now. Get off the roads. Emergency vehicles only. Seek shelter immediately. Over."

Elena could see the dust had thickened. Curious, she
opened her door and stepped outside, throwing an arm
across her nose and mouth. A dry wind whipped her hair
around her face, and she could hear the flags near the
Commander's office snapping against the metal poles.
She looked toward the east and gasped. An enormous
billowing cloud of dust rolled slowly toward her. The
cloud towered over the base, at least sixty feet high,
and the leading edge bloomed outward like a nuclear
explosion in slow motion.

Elena stared, hypnotized.

"Ma'am, please remain indoors." The Humvee had
stopped directly in front of her unit, and Elena could
see a soldier in the driver's seat speaking to her through
a handheld unit that broadcasted out of a speaker on

the roof. Elena nodded jerkily and, with a last look at the advancing cloud, ducked back inside and closed the door.

It was just a dust storm, she reminded herself. There was nothing dangerous about it, yet she felt anxious and edgy. She stood at the window and watched the cloud advance until suddenly, the sun vanished and the entire housing area was swallowed up in a thick, reddish haze. In the space of a heartbeat, daylight turned to complete darkness.

Elena fumbled for the lights, switching on the small utility lamps over the desk and bed. Back home, she'd always enjoyed a good thunderstorm or snowstorm, but this was unlike anything she'd experienced before. The wind whistled past the door, and an occasional burst of gravel and sand rattled against the window. She almost wished she was still in her former CHU, where at least she'd have the company of the female soldiers. She could envision them joking and playing cards, or lounging on their cots listening to their iPods.

Knowing that she wouldn't get any more work done while the storm raged through the base, she gave up any pretense of doing so and lay down on her bed to read one of the paperbacks she'd brought with her. She'd barely gotten through the first chapter, however, when the lights flickered, and then went out altogether, plunging her small living space into complete blackness. The air-conditioning unit whirred to a stop, and the only sound was the wind.

Elena sat up, heart pounding, and waited. And just like Chase had promised, there was a mechanical snap, and the overhead utility light came on, casting the room in an eerie bluish glow. Elena had spent her entire adult life living alone and she'd always enjoyed having her own space, but now she would have given anything for the sound of another human voice.

The emergency lighting was insufficient to read by, so Elena flopped back on her bed and closed her eyes, listening to the lonely sound of the wind. Before long, she grew uncomfortably warm, and realized the air conditioner had not restarted when the back-up generators had kicked in. Which made perfect sense, since they drew so much electricity. But the heat inside the trailer was quickly becoming oppressive and Elena didn't even have the option of cracking a window.

Standing up, she opened another bottle of water and sipped it, but found no relief from the cloying warmth. She wondered if it was possible to suffocate from lack of air movement, and if she might not be better off trying to make her way to the dining hall or the small recreation center, where at least there would be other people around. But a quick glance out the window told her that, if anything, the dust storm had only intensified. She'd be lucky if she could see her hand in front of her face. Finding her way to the street, never mind to the dining facility, would be next to impossible.

There was no question in her mind that she was stuck in her quarters for however long the storm lasted. With a sigh she peeled off her uniform until she wore only her bra and underwear, and then grabbed her iPod and lay down on her bed to wait it out. At least with the strains of Coldplay in her ears, she could shut out the lonely sound of the wind. And if she closed her eyes, she could almost imagine she was somewhere else.

What was Chase doing right now? Was he with his team, planning his next mission? Did he think about her? Her mind drifted back to that moment in the MRAP when he'd almost kissed her. She'd known he was going to, and the knowledge had thrilled her. Her heart had begun racing the second he'd crouched in front of her to help adjust the bandana. She'd wanted to inhale him, to absorb him through her skin. But she'd seen a small red light by the door begin to blink the second before the door had swung open, and she'd quickly moved away.

She knew instinctively that the reason Chase had asked Mike and Pete to bring her the food and water was because he didn't trust himself to be alone with her.

Smart guy.

While she'd been unwilling to compromise his reputation in front of his men, there would have been nothing to prevent her from completely seducing him in the privacy of her living quarters. But she also knew he wouldn't stay away. Eventually, he'd come by to make sure she was okay because that's the kind of guy he was. And when he did, she'd be waiting.

12

A SOFT WHOOSH, followed by a low, deep thump that shook the ground, had the men of the 2nd Marines Special Operations Battalion scrambling for their body armor.

"Holy shit," exclaimed Lego, tightening his helmet strap beneath his chin, "that sucker sounded like it hit the compound!"

Chase and the others had been waiting out the dust storm by scrupulously going over the upcoming mission and ensuring their backup plans were in place in the event it turned into a complete disaster.

Now Chase shot to his feet and flung open the door of the Tac Ops building, trying to see where the mortar had hit. The worst of the dust storm had passed, but the air was thick with a choking red haze that would linger for days, making visibility almost impossible. Night was falling, although it was difficult to tell, given the heavy fog of dust that enveloped the base.

Stepping outside, he could see a darker cloud of smoke and fumes from the area of the motor pool. "Looks like we took a direct hit on the eastern side of the base," he yelled over his shoulder. Even as he spoke, there came another low, howling whistle.

"Jesus!" shouted Sean. "Incoming!"

In the same instant, the mortar hit with an explosive thud, only closer this time, near the dining facility. The ground beneath Chase's feet trembled with the impact. Immediately, the sirens began to wail, and there was pandemonium as soldiers scrambled to get to their battle stations or to a bunker. The air was filled with the sound of voices as men shouted orders and directions.

Chase heard a low, distant *whoompf* and knew another mortar had just been launched. *Elena.* He had to get to Elena. She'd be terrified, alone in her trailer. He'd told her that if there was an attack, to get her ass to the nearest bunker, but with the choking dust, he wasn't sure she'd be able to find her way.

Without hesitating, he leaped down the steps and began sprinting toward the housing area, ignoring the shouts of his men to come back. The third mortar hit somewhere just outside the compound wall, but close enough that the impact made him stumble. Regaining his footage, he ran on, searching the faces of those who passed him in the other direction, hoping that he'd see Elena. But there were only soldiers, racing toward the bunkers and their stations. He reached Elena's CHU and tried the door handle, but found it locked.

"Elena!" he shouted, knowing the likelihood of her hearing him over the wail of the sirens was slim to none. "Elena!"

There was no response, and he wondered if she might actually have listened to him and already left for the bomb shelter. But she wouldn't have locked her door behind her, which meant she was still inside. Standing back, he used his foot to kick the door in and then he was inside her quarters, moving swiftly through the empty living area and into her bedroom.

"Elena, what the hell are you doing?" Relief at seeing her sitting uninjured on the edge of her bed washed over him, making his voice rougher than he'd intended.

She'd donned her protective vest and her helmet, and was struggling to pull her boots onto her bare feet. Now she looked up at him, her eyes enormous.

"I—I just need to get my boots on," she explained shakily, "and then I'm leaving."

"Too damned late for that," he growled, and bent to haul her to her feet. "You should have been gone ten seconds after those sirens sounded. Christ!"

To his astonishment she twisted her arm free and turned back to the bed. "I need to put my boots on," she said stubbornly. "I can't run in my bare feet."

"Then I'll goddamned well carry you," he all but shouted, "but we need to go *now.*"

Before she could protest, he bent a shoulder beneath her and lifted her over his back, holding her in place with one hand across the back of her thighs and—*Jesus!* Beneath the armored vest she wore nothing but a pair of panties, and his palm rested solidly against soft, warm skin. He realized that she must have been sleeping when the attack occurred.

Now she struggled in his grasp, pushing herself upright as she clutched at his shoulders. "No, wait!" she panted. "I need my boots! I can't go out there without my boots!"

"Elena—"

"Put me down!"

He could carry her even if she struggled, but it

wouldn't be pleasant for her or for him, so he put her down, prepared to reason with her and yes, even let her put her damned boots on if that's what it took to get her to a bunker.

But the moment he set her on her feet, another whooshing sound came from overhead. Instinctively, Chase pushed Elena to the floor and covered her with his body. The impact, when it came, was dangerously close, rattling the windows of the little hut and shaking the walls. Almost immediately, the mortar was followed by the sounds of a counterattack as the U.S. troops fired back, launching their own missiles in the direction of the insurgency.

As Chase covered Elena, he became aware of several things at once. The first was that while Elena wore both a flak vest and helmet, he'd charged out of the Tac Ops building with neither. In fact, he was damn near as naked as Elena was, wearing only a pair of shorts and T-shirt. The air-conditioning had quit when the power went out, and when the heat had become too oppressive, he and his men had changed into casual clothes. To have gone sprinting across the base during a mortar attack without his protective gear had been beyond stupid. Christ, he knew better!

In the next instant, he became aware of Elena, curled on the floor beneath him. She hadn't fastened her helmet and it had fallen off when she'd hit the deck. Now his nostrils were filled with the scent of her flowery shampoo. The armored inserts of her flak vest dug into his chest and stomach where he pressed her against the floor, but her legs—her smooth, bare legs—were tangled with his.

The mortars had stopped although the sirens still

wailed. Chase lifted his head and looked down at Elena. Her eyes were tightly closed.

"Elena," he said, smoothing her hair back. "Elena, look at me."

She did, opening her eyes to stare at him, and he saw the fear in her eyes and for a split second he thought she was afraid of *him*.

"Oh, Chase," she whispered, and she flung her arms around his neck, clutching him as if she'd never let go. "I was so frightened."

"I know, baby, I know," he whispered back, emotion roughening his voice. He pushed into a sitting position with his back against her bed and pulled her across his lap, cradling her head against his shoulder. "But it's okay now. In a minute the sirens will stop, and this will all be over."

She shuddered and burrowed closer. "I wanted to leave, but I couldn't find my protective gear and you said I shouldn't leave unless I was wearing it, but then I was barefoot and I couldn't get my boots on."

"Shh," he soothed. "It's okay. You're safe now. Listen." He cocked his head. "The sirens have stopped."

Elena raised her head and as they listened, the sirens let out several short blasts.

"Hear that?" he asked softly, keeping his voice low. "That's the all-clear sign. It's over."

"Thank God," she breathed. "I never want to go through something like that ever again."

Chase pressed his lips against her hair, knowing this was a perfect opportunity to suggest she return to Kuwait or even the States, but he selfishly kept his mouth shut. He didn't want her to leave, even though he knew it was dangerous for her to stay. He tried to convince himself that he only wanted her near so that he could keep an eye on her, but that was a lie.

He wanted her near because he was a selfish bastard.

Because he just plain wanted her.

"Is the dust storm over?" she asked.

"Mostly. The wind has died down, but the air is still pretty thick. They should have the main power back on in a few hours."

"A sandstorm and a mortar attack, all in one day," she said, laughing a little. "They'll never believe this back home."

"I should have expected it," Chase said grimly. "The insurgents like to launch their attacks during bad weather. They know our options for retaliating are limited. Hey." He cupped her face and pulled back enough to look at her, smoothing his thumbs over her cheeks. "You okay?"

She drew in a deep breath and nodded. "I am now."

They stared at each other for a long moment until hot color seeped into her face and she looked down. "Oh, wow," she exclaimed in mortification. "I should put some clothes on."

"No, you're fine," Chase protested, reluctant to let her go. Reluctant to have her cover up all the warm, feminine flesh pressed against him.

She gave him a tolerant look. "Somehow, I don't think a flak vest falls under the category of *clothing*."

He released her and she braced her hands on his shoulders to push herself up, but then stopped. Her eyes traveled over him, taking in his T-shirt, shorts and bare legs, before flying back to his face.

"You're not wearing protective gear." Her voice was

filled with a combination of horror and wonder. "You came over here without even putting on your helmet."

He knew his expression was chagrined. "I didn't have time," he said carefully.

"But you're like the King of Combat Rules," she persisted. "The only thing that kept me from running, screaming, out of this building the second those mortars hit, was what would happen to me if you caught me without my helmet and vest, and yet you..." Her words drifted off.

"Like I said, I didn't have time." His tone was gruff.

"Because you were worried about me." Her gaze was filled with dawning understanding. "You broke one of your own hard, fast rules because you were worried for my safety."

Chase started to protest that he absolutely had *not* abandoned protocol because of her, but the expression on her face caused the words to die on his lips. She looked stunned. And awed. Like he was her own personal hero.

And just like that, he broke. "I couldn't get here fast enough," he admitted, his voice hoarse with recalled fear. He cupped her face in his hands, searching her eyes. "The thought of anything happening to you..."

"Oh, Chase," she breathed, and then she was kissing him. But Jesus, she wasn't just kissing him, she was *devouring* him. Chase resisted for about a nanosecond because as much as he'd dreamed of this happening, this was not the reason he'd raced across the compound during a mortar attack. He'd just needed to make sure Elena was okay and maybe stay long enough to comfort her. But this worked, too.

Elena raised herself up and straddled his thighs, holding his face in her hands as she angled her mouth across his. Her tongue swept past his lips, and Chase groaned. His arms went around her, and he realized she still wore her flak vest.

"Let's get this off," he managed, his fingers working the Velcro fastenings. She helped him slide it off, and then there she was, wearing nothing but a lacy white bra.

"Oh, man," he groaned, "you are so damned beautiful."

Elena wound her arms around his neck and he buried his face in her neck, breathing in her scent. She smelled like shampoo and soap and under that, a subtly feminine smell that was hers alone. The combination was a complete turn-on.

"Take this off," she demanded, tugging at his shirt, and he helped her push it up and over his head until finally—proof that there really was a God—they were skin on skin.

He wanted to consume her, to take her hard and fast and deep, until she acknowledged that she was his. The mortar attack, combined with the adrenaline rush of fear he'd felt for Elena's safety, had left him completely jacked. He couldn't remember the last time he'd ached so desperately for sexual release. Well, that wasn't completely true; he'd been in serious pain after he'd pushed her away in the men's showers. He was rock-hard for her, but there was a minuscule part of his brain that still functioned.

"Elena, babe," he managed, "we can't do this. There are rules—"

"Too bad, soldier," she breathed, shifting so that she

was in full, sweet contact with his erection. "Some rules were meant to be broken."

And then she kissed him, a hot, openmouthed kiss that made him forget his rule about no sex on the base. Jesus, he should stop, he knew that, but she made him forget everything except his need to be with her, inside her, hearing her gasps of pleasure as he pushed her over the edge.

She was fumbling with his zipper and he flicked the fastening of her bra open, filling his hands with her breasts. He stood up, pulling her with him, and helped her to strip off his shorts even as he pushed her panties down, and then they were both gloriously naked. He wanted to inhale her, to run his hands and mouth over every inch of her and reassure himself that she really was okay.

Chase lay back on the narrow bed, pulling her down on top of him, and she laughed as she kissed him again, their teeth scraping together before he swept his tongue into her mouth. She was liquid fire in his arms, her sleek, warm thighs pressed tightly against either side of his hips as she rocked against him, her fingers in his hair, her soft breasts crushed against his chest.

When she reached between their bodies and curled her fingers around him, he had to grit his teeth to force himself not to come immediately.

"Oh, God," she panted, lifting her head to gaze down at him, "you're so *hard*. And hot."

Oh, yeah. The things she was doing made his eyes roll back, but when she raised herself up to position him at the entrance to her body, he reacted swiftly.

"Whoa, babe!" Before she could lower herself onto his straining cock, he flipped her so that she lay beneath him on the narrow bed, her legs still curled around his hips. "I didn't exactly come prepared for this," he explained, seeing her confusion. "I don't have any protection."

She swallowed hard, and he could see indecision warring with desire in her shimmering eyes. "Well, I'm on the Pill," she finally admitted. "And I promise you that I don't have anything contagious or dangerous."

Chase might have argued that, since he was pretty sure everything about her, including her smile, was dangerous to his heart, but he wasn't a man to question good fortune.

"I just had a full battery of tests and all my shots before I came over here," he said, not adding that he hadn't had sex with anyone but her since before the *last* time he'd deployed, about eighteen months ago. "I'm squeaky-clean."

Elena searched his eyes and gave him a smile that caused his heart to turn over in his chest. "Well, except for the dust," she said, wiping a single finger along his jaw and showing him the reddish evidence on its tip. "Please, I don't want to wait anymore."

As if to emphasize her words, she arched upward, pressing herself against him. Chase groaned and she caught his face in her hands, covering his mouth in another soul-destroying kiss. But when she would have reached between their bodies to touch him, he pushed her hands over her head and held them there. He didn't know how long he could last if she touched him again.

He dipped his head and kissed one breast, then drew her nipple into his mouth. Elena gasped. Chase smiled and released her wrists to slide his hand down her body and along the back of her thigh, lifting her leg higher and hooking it behind his back, opening her to him.

He slid his aching cock against her, feeling how warm and slick she was, and wanted nothing more than to bury himself in her heat.

"Elena," he rasped, "I thought I could go slow, but I'm not sure I can…"

"I don't want you to go slow," she said, pressing her hips upward. "I want you inside me now."

Chase wanted the same thing, but his control was tenuous, at best, and he was afraid he'd lose it too soon. He eased himself into her, inch by excruciating inch, stretching and filling her, gritting his teeth against the overwhelming urge to thrust hard and deep and fast.

God. God, he could hardly stand it.

"Jesus, I've never done this without a condom," he said thickly.

"Me, either," she whispered, and arched upward, gasping his name, clutching his back and urging him closer. "Is this considered preferential treatment?"

"Oh, yeah," he groaned.

And then he was fully seated inside her, surrounded by her silky heat, and he could feel the walls of her sex gripping him. She began to move, rocking against him. Chase rested his head against her neck and pushed deeper, and she rose up to meet him. Elena made a strangled sound of pleasure and cried his name, and that's all it took for Chase to lose whatever restraint he had.

He thrust into her, harder, again and again, and the small sounds she made drove him over the edge, shattering his control, but it was okay because she was there, too, coming apart in his arms. His heart pounded like a jackhammer in his chest, and one coherent thought managed to surface in his lust-saturated brain.

They didn't make body armor tough enough to protect his heart from this woman.

13

ELENA LAY WITH HER HEAD on Chase's chest, listening to the heavy thump of his heart beneath her ear. She wrapped her arms tighter around him, never wanting him to leave. Lying with him like this, she could almost forget where they were, or that they'd just survived a mortar attack.

"Did you actually kick my door in?" she asked, recalling how he'd burst into her quarters.

"Hmm? What?"

He was almost asleep and now he came partially awake, his eyes reflecting his confusion.

"I'm pretty sure I locked my door earlier," she said, tracing a finger over his chest, "so I just wanted to ask if you really kicked it in?"

"Holy f—" He broke off abruptly and sat up, disentangling himself from Elena's arms.

She sat up, too, pushing her hair back and watching as he snatched his shorts from the floor and shoved his legs into them.

"What's wrong?"

"How long have I been here? Did I fall asleep? Shit,

shit, *shit!*" He searched the floor, found his T-shirt and dragged it on, then began looking for his sandals. "They'll be doing a head count, and I should be back at Tac Ops, and they'll be wondering where the hell I disappeared to and—*shit!*"

Elena had never seen him like this—out of control. Even when he'd been angry, he'd never used such foul language. She found her panties and pulled them on, and then grabbed a clean shirt from the shelf next to the bed.

"You didn't tell anyone that you were coming here?" she asked, incredulous. Even she knew that you didn't just disappear during an emergency. She'd assumed he'd told *somebody* where he was headed. "You just left?"

"Can you believe that?" he asked, laughing in disbelief. "I should know better. Jesus! I should be out there with my men, doing damage control and helping to launch a counterattack, and instead I'm in here—" He broke off abruptly. "Where's my damned sandal?"

Elena stood up, understanding that his anger was directed at himself and not at her. He'd broken another rule, again because of her. But she couldn't feel sorry for what they'd done. Bending down, she retrieved his sandal from where it lay beneath her flak vest and handed it to him.

He took it from her silently. She thought he would just go, but he stood there for a moment, turning the shoe over in his hand.

"Elena," he began.

She laid her fingers over his lips. "Shh. Don't say anything, okay?"

Because if he told her that he regretted what had just happened between them, she'd lose it. And she'd been working so hard to show him that she was tough and capable, and could handle being out here just as well as he could. But if he said that being with her was a mistake, she might just cry.

"I'm sorry," he muttered. "This has nothing to do with you." He turned away, rubbing a hand across the back of his neck. When he turned back to her, she could see that he was back in control. "Coming over to make sure you were okay was one thing, but taking advantage of you like that was another thing altogether."

Elena stared at him. "You think you took advantage of me?"

"I do. I did. You were scared and I only meant to reassure you, but instead I completely used your vulnerability to my own advantage."

Elena smiled. "You didn't hear me complaining, did you?"

Chase returned her smile, but it didn't reach his eyes. "Listen, I hate to do this, but I really do have to run."

"I understand."

"Elena…" He hesitated.

"I know," she said, not wanting to hear him say it. "This can't happen again." To her relief, she didn't cry. She wrapped her arms around her middle, hugging herself. "There are rules against this sort of thing. I get it."

"If there's another attack, I'll send one of the female soldiers to bring you to the bunker."

"There's no need," she said quickly, keeping her voice even. "I know the drill now. I know what to expect, and I'll be fine."

Boy, did she ever know the drill. She could have Chase for stolen moments here and there, but he'd never let his guard down enough to really be hers. Not on a permanent basis.

He looked uncertain, and Elena almost felt a stab of sympathy for him. God, next he was going to apologize, and she didn't know if she could handle that. Because she couldn't feel the tiniest bit sorry about what they'd done.

"Go," she said. "Just…go."

He did.

THE MORTAR ATTACK had done minimal damage to the base and there were no casualties, unless you counted the Humvee parked in the motor pool. Elena had seen the truck and there were so many ragged holes torn in the doors and roof that it resembled Swiss cheese.

But the attack had left the compound in a state of heightened alert, and even Corporal Cleary and Sergeant Corrente were too focused on their jobs to give her anything more than a cursory greeting in passing.

There was a surreal quality to the base in the days immediately following. The dust storm had passed, but the air was still heavy and thick with a reddish haze that even the sun couldn't completely penetrate. Routine patrols were on hold since visibility was so poor. As a result, most of the soldiers were confined to the base and kept busy doing maintenance and repair on everything from the buildings and fences to the vehicles.

Elena was busy, too. She spent the next two days in the contracting center with Brad, ensuring the minor damage to the dining facility was repaired, expediting delivery of the parts needed to complete the waste treatment plant and keeping needed supplies flowing into the base.

She didn't see Chase, although she found herself looking for him whenever she walked between her office or the dining facility and her housing unit. She didn't even know if he was still on the base, or if he and his men had gone out on patrol into the surrounding hills. She had sat in on the post-attack briefings, knew the Taliban were responsible for the mortar attack on the base, and that the U.S. forces had retaliated with enough firepower to smoke the entire mountain where the explosives had been launched from. During the day, she tried not to think about him or what he might be doing or whether he was safe. Or if he thought of her.

But at night, in her solitary living quarters, she couldn't escape her memories of their time together, both in Kuwait and following the attack. She'd been so certain when he'd been with her, loving her with his body, that it had been more than just a physical joining for him. She hadn't imagined the sheer relief she'd seen on his face when he'd found her alive and whole, or the desperation in his touch as he'd made love to her.

She knew he considered his attraction to her a weakness. He didn't bend the rules for anyone, and he'd said more than once that he wouldn't give her preferential treatment. Yet he'd gone out of his way to ensure her comfort and her safety. He'd personally accompanied her to the drilling site. He'd given her his CHU. Surely that meant something?

"Hey, why don't you call it a day?"

Elena looked up from her computer to see Brad Carrington standing in the doorway to her little office. He was handsome, in his own way, with red hair, blue eyes and fair skin that was perpetually sunburned. To Elena, he looked like a slightly older version of Prince Harry. His smile was friendly enough, and he worked just as hard as Elena did, even if he refused to go outside the fence to visit any of their projects.

"I'm a navy guy," he'd said more than once. "I don't play in sandboxes."

Elena understood that unlike her, the Defense Procurement Agency hadn't given him any choice about coming over to Afghanistan. He'd taken a three-year assignment with the DPA because he'd wanted to be at home with his wife and kids instead of having to be at sea for months at a time. But then they'd sent him to Afghanistan for a year and he wasn't at all happy about it.

"I'm just wrapping up this e-mail," Elena said, "and then I'm calling it a night."

"You've been at it for almost fourteen hours," Brad said. "Tomorrow is Sunday. You should sleep in."

Elena smiled at him. "Maybe I will." She wouldn't.

"It's dark outside. You want me to walk you back to your quarters?"

If the offer had come from anyone but Brad, Elena might have interpreted it as a come-on, but she knew without a doubt that the navy officer was completely devoted to the wife he'd left in San Diego.

"I'll be fine," she assured him. "But I did want to ask you if I could arrange to go back out to the drilling site?"

Brad frowned. "You were just out there. Why do you need to go back?"

"I want to check on the progress they're making laying the pipeline from the well to the base."

"Is that really necessary? Can't you just talk with the project manager about it? Going out there isn't safe."

Elena gave him a tolerant look. "It's less than two

miles from the base, and I'll only be gone for a couple of hours. I just received an invoice for more than a million dollars for the work they've done just this past month. The invoice states they've laid three hundred meters of pipeline, which I find hard to believe. Before I authorize payment, I'd like to verify the progress myself." She shrugged. "It's part of my job, Brad."

He sighed. "Well, okay, if you have to. I'll talk with Charlie Company and see if they can set you up with an escort. When did you want to go?"

"As soon as it can be arranged."

"I'll see what I can do. I'd feel a lot better if one of the special ops guys could go with you, like the last time, but that's not a possibility now."

He had Elena's full attention, although she tried to sound casual. "Why is that?"

"They're leaving tonight."

Elena felt her heart tighten. "Are you sure?"

"Yep."

Elena didn't ask him how he knew. As one of the few officers on the base, there probably wasn't much that went on that he didn't know about. She strove to sound natural, when inside she was freaking out. Chase was leaving on a mission that she knew would be dangerous. "How long will they be gone?"

"Until they've completed whatever mission they've been assigned. They're usually gone for a week or two, at least."

A week or two. Logically, she knew a couple of weeks was not a long time, but to Elena it felt like an eternity. Chase was preparing to leave and he hadn't even bothered to let her know or say goodbye. But what had she expected? A declaration of love? A promise of forever?

Not when their relationship had started as a one-night stand.

She felt sick. More than that, she felt angry. Angry at Chase for not caring enough to say goodbye, and angry at herself for caring too much.

After Brad left, Elena finished her e-mail and closed her computer. Glancing at her watch, she saw it was 8:00 p.m. Her chest felt tight and ached. She pressed her fingers against her eyes, trying to think rationally.

Chase was leaving.

She shouldn't feel so hurt that he hadn't told her, but when she recalled his face the last time she'd seen him, she wanted to cry. He might want her, but he resented the hell out of her, too. She represented everything he believed was wrong with the military—she was female and she was in a combat environment. Worse, she was a civilian. She didn't even have the benefit of a military background or training. He probably viewed his attraction to her as a colossal weakness in his character.

Sighing, Elena pushed away from her desk and retrieved her flak vest and helmet. She was completely wired, which meant she'd lie in bed tossing and turning, thinking about Chase and aching for him. She'd never been so attuned to the needs of her own body as she'd been since she met Chase. All she had to do was think about him and her body would begin to thrum with recalled pleasure. And unless she was engrossed in her work, she thought about him pretty much all the time.

Snapping off the lights in the office, she locked the door and turned to walk to her living quarters when a lone figure detached itself from the shadows and approached her.

Elena hesitated. While she hadn't heard of any women

being attacked on the base, she wasn't naive enough to think it couldn't happen. She stood uncertainly for a moment, torn between flight or fight, when the man stepped closer and she recognized Chase.

"Oh, my God," she gasped, her body sagging in relief. "You scared me there for a moment."

"Why are you walking back alone?" he demanded, grasping her by the arms and giving her a light shake. "It's not safe."

"Brad offered to walk with me, but I refused," she explained, trying to discern his expression in the indistinct light. Her heart had exploded into a frenzied rhythm as soon as she saw him, and now she strove to sound normal, as if seeing him didn't upset her equilibrium. "What are *you* doing out here?"

"I was waiting for you." He released her arms and took a step back, as if he didn't trust himself to get too close.

"Oh."

"And why aren't you wearing your protective gear?" He took her vest from her hands and held it out for her to slip into. "Jesus, please don't tell me you go outside without it, not after the other night?"

"I'm only going to my quarters and it's so heavy," she explained, knowing that was a poor excuse. "I hate wearing it."

"Well, get used to it," he said grimly. "Most mortar attacks occur between eight and ten o'clock. You should wear it whenever you're outside."

Elena wasn't in the mood to talk about what would happen if the base came under another attack; the last one was still fresh in her mind. And she wasn't the only one who was thinking about that night. She could see from Chase's expression that he was remembering what had happened, too.

"Is that why you're here?" she asked. "To make sure I'm wearing my protective gear? Jeez, Chase, I'm a big girl. I can take care of myself." Irritated with herself for being glad that he cared, that he had come to see her before he left, she pushed past him and strode in the direction of her living quarters.

He fell into step beside her and they walked in silence until they reached her door. He blew out a hard breath. "Listen, there's something I need to tell you. We can talk inside...or maybe that's not such a good idea."

A foot patrol of two soldiers turned the corner at the end of the road, walking toward them, and Elena made a quick decision. "No, it's okay," she said quietly. "Come in. I can make some coffee, if you'd like."

"I can't stay long."

He stood back while she unlocked the door and flipped on the light, and then followed her inside, closing the door behind them. Elena slipped out of her vest and dropped it onto a chair. Turning toward Chase, she got her first good look at him.

He looked dangerous.

His face was covered in several days' growth of beard, making his chiseled cheekbones stand out even more prominently. She realized he wasn't wearing the traditional desert camo fatigues that she'd become accustomed to seeing him in. Both his pants and his jacket were solid beige beneath his heavy vest, and he wore a black-and-white checkered scarf wrapped around his neck. A patch on one arm bore the initials *NKA*.

"Why are you dressed like that?" she asked.

"I'm leaving tonight."

She already knew, but hearing him say the words caused her heart to twist painfully. "Where are you going?"

"I'm sorry, I can't say. All I can tell you is that I'll be gone for a week or so, but I didn't want to leave without telling you."

He had come to say goodbye. And just like that, the hurt and anger evaporated. Was this what it was like for military wives and girlfriends each time their husbands or lovers deployed? She felt weak with fear for Chase. She was unfamiliar with the painful, clenching sensation in her chest, or the way she couldn't seem to catch her breath.

Unwilling to let him see her weakness, she turned away to open the Tupperware container of coffee and scoop some into the coffeemaker. Her hands trembled, and she finally dropped the spoon back into the container and braced her hands on the shelves, her head down. "I can't do this," she whispered.

"Elena." He was right behind her.

"Don't." She was only barely holding it together.

"Elena, look at me." His voice was low and insistent.

He turned her around, and she knew couldn't hide the tears that had welled in her eyes, so she tried to laugh them off.

"I'm sorry," she said, smiling as she wiped at her eyes, "You just took me by surprise."

"I'll be fine," he said softly, studying her face. "This is my job. It's what I do."

"I know." She nodded, trying to sound strong. "I do."

"Ah, babe, come here."

Before she could protest, he hauled her into his arms and she went willingly, winding her arms around his waist and pressing her face against his chest. She felt his lips against her hair, and then he tipped her face up so that he could look at her.

"You'll be okay while I'm gone?" he asked.

She pushed back and stared at him, letting her gaze drift over his face, lingering on his mouth.

"Listen to yourself." Her voice sounded strained. "You're the one going into a dangerous situation, and yet here you are, asking me if *I'll* be okay?"

"I can't be distracted by worrying about you," he admitted, "but I know I'll worry anyway. Just promise me that you won't leave the base, and that you'll wear your protective gear and do everything you're supposed to do to keep safe while I'm gone. *Promise.*"

Elena felt more tears well in her eyes. It wasn't a declaration of love, but she suspected this was the closest thing she'd get from Chase.

For now.

She stood on tiptoe and he cupped her face in his hands and kissed her so sweetly, so tenderly, that she prayed to God to keep him safe. Just watch over him and bring him back safely, and she would never, ever ask for anything more than this moment. Please, God, do this one thing, and when the time came—and she knew it would—she would let him go.

14

FROM THE HELICOPTER, Chase saw Forward Operating Base Sharlana come into view. He watched as a small convoy of vehicles left the base and wondered where it was headed. After ten days away, he and his team were finally back. The helicopter was coming in low, preparing to land, and he could make out every structure. There was the housing area, and there was the roof of Elena's CHU. The sun had barely risen; was she still sleeping, or had she already left for work?

He was impatient to get onto the ground. As exhausted and filthy as he was, he had just one driving need—to see Elena. He could try and tell himself that he just wanted to make sure she was safe, but he knew he was full of shit.

The woman had gotten under his skin in a big way. As much as he told himself that he didn't want her on the base, he had to admire the way she'd adapted. She hadn't freaked out during the sandstorm or the mortar attack, and she wasn't afraid to leave the protection of the base to visit the construction sites. Moreover, she'd shown herself to be adept at her job, and he'd overheard several officers speaking highly of her skills. All in all, he was pretty amazed by her tenacity and proud as hell of her courage.

He glanced away from the window to the other four members of his team, wondering if he looked as rough and weary as they did. After ten days spent crawling through the rugged mountains, they looked more like enemy insurgents than they did American soldiers. He hadn't showered, his beard had grown in and scratched uncomfortably against his skin, his uniform was soiled and torn in places, and he'd lost weight.

But they'd succeeded in intercepting the weapons transfer and had captured not only Mullah Abdul Raqid, but two of his top advisers, as well. The operation had been an unmitigated success, especially when Chase considered the information they'd found out from Raqid's men.

He just needed to get on the ground and brief the base commander so Colonel Vinson could prevent any troops from inadvertently traveling into the area where the Taliban was planning an ambush. They hadn't been able to convey that information over the radio for fear of giving away their position or having the enemy intercept the communication. He needed to tell the commander in person. Then he'd clean himself up and head over to Elena's quarters. There were no rules in existence that could keep him from spending the next twenty-four hours in her arms, and his body tightened in anticipation.

As soon as they landed, Chase jumped down from the helicopter, bending low beneath the rotors as he and his men jogged over to a waiting Humvee.

Climbing inside, he was surprised to see the colonel

sitting in the passenger's seat. Great. If they could debrief him on the way to Tac Ops, he could shave a few minutes off the time it would take to get to Elena's.

"Gentlemen," Vinson said, turning in his seat to face the team. "Welcome back and congratulations on a job well done. Your efforts reflect favorably not only on yourselves, but on the U.S. Marine Corps. Your last communication said you had information regarding a potential ambush. Tell me what you know."

"Thank you, sir," replied Rafe. "The detainees are on their way to Kabul under armed escort, but we do have information that we believe is reliable and may impact your operations here at Sharlana."

The prisoners had confessed that one of the nearby villages had been harboring a dozen or more insurgents and that these same insurgents were planning to ambush the next military convoy that traveled through the village. Chase couldn't help but think about the similar ambush during his last deployment in Iraq.

The memory of the female convoy driver getting shot still haunted him. Try as he might, he would never be comfortable putting women in harm's way.

Rafe was still talking to the commander, and Chase forced himself to concentrate on their conversation. The tiny village of Jani didn't exist on any map, and U.S. troops rarely passed through the hamlet. The route to the drilling site came close to Jani, but in order to actually drive through the village, a convoy would have to leave the main road and make a circuitous detour. And the only reason a convoy would use the detour would be if the main road became impassable—

Chase leaned forward. "Sir, I saw a convoy of

MRAPs leaving the base as we were flying in. Where is it headed?"

The men waited as the commander picked up the radio and spoke to the motor pool. The response made Chase go cold.

"Sir, convoy is headed to the southeast drilling site. Over."

"Find out if any civilians are with that convoy," Chase said tightly. "Ask if Elena de la Vega is in one of those trucks."

"Roger that," came the reply. "That's an affirmative. Over."

"Shit!" Chase wanted to punch something. He felt impotent. Elena was in one of those vehicles and if, as he suspected, the main road had been rendered impassable, the MRAPs would have two choices—they could turn back and return to the base, or they could make a detour through the village of Jani, where they could be ambushed by the Taliban.

He hoped like hell they decided to turn back. How long had it been since he'd seen the convoy leave? Ten minutes? Twelve, at most? Enough time to have reached the turnoff to Jani.

"Colonel, I'm going to need this vehicle," Chase said grimly.

The colonel nodded. "You can have my driver, as well. I'll come with you."

"Sorry, sir," Rafe said, "but with all due respect, we can't allow that. We'll drop you off here, if that works."

The commander sighed. "I guess it'll have to. Be careful, boys, and good luck. I'll get you some backup and some air support."

They dropped the commander off by the motor pool, and then they were racing out of the base toward the drilling site. Chase couldn't believe that Elena had actually left the base after she'd promised not to. He should have anticipated that the Taliban would eventually try to attack a convoy traveling to the drilling site. Knowing that Elena was part of that convoy made his blood run cold. For once, he hoped the information they'd received was false. He hoped that they'd arrive at the drilling site to find Elena drinking lemonade with the project manager. The alternative was unthinkable.

Chase scanned the road as the Humvee sped along, taking the curves too fast, in danger of overturning if they miscalculated even a little. But the driver, a kid barely out of his teens, seemed imperturbable as he maneuvered the rutted road, and Chase eyeballed him with respect. "Nice driving," he murmured.

The kid flashed a grin without taking his eyes from the road. "Everything I know about driving I learned on the back roads of Alabama. Nothing like being underage with a trunk full of beer and three cop cars in pursuit to hone your driving skills."

"Very nice," approved Rafe, his eyes gleaming.

"There!" Chase indicated the road. "Slow down. The road is out up ahead."

A rockfall from the nearby hill made the road impassable, and the deep ditch on the other side made circling around the barrier impossible. Chase felt his heart come into his throat. There was no way the convoy could have gotten around the debris, and they hadn't encountered any trucks since they'd left the base. Which meant the convoy had taken the alternate route through the village of Jani.

Sean leaned forward to get a better look, surveying the hillside with critical eyes. "Natural or man-made?" he asked, referring to the fallen debris.

"We have to assume it's man-made, and that the insurgents are counting on that convoy taking the detour and passing through Jani. Back it up," Chase said to the driver. "The turnoff is just behind us."

They backed up and took the turnoff to Jani, and up ahead, Chase could just make out a low cloud of dust. "That must be them. Slow down, and keep your eyes open."

As one, the men readied their weapons. Chase surveyed the landscape on either side of the road, noting the thick copse of trees on one side and the steep hill, studded with boulders, on the other. Even now, insurgents could be hiding on either side of the road, aiming their weapons at the convoy.

The dusty road was narrow and deeply rutted, and as they rounded a curve, Chase had a clear view of the three MRAPs. They had come to a stop about a hundred meters from the village.

"Jesus Christ," he breathed, and his blood ran cold.

Elena and two soldiers had exited their vehicle and were walking toward the front of the convoy. And approaching them from the village was a group of men, dressed in long, loose traditional clothing. Clothing that could conceal anything from rifles to grenades. What the hell were Elena and the soldiers thinking? Didn't they understand the danger they were in? Chase realized he had stopped breathing as he braced himself for the sound of gunfire. He needed to reach Elena before that happened—to protect her with his own body, if need be.

In that instant, Chase realized he would do anything to keep her safe. Even die.

The Humvee skidded to a stop behind the last MRAP, and Chase had to force himself not to leap out at a dead run. The last thing he wanted was to startle the local men and inadvertently instigate a firefight before Elena was safely back in the MRAP. He'd have those soldiers' balls in a vice for letting her out of the vehicle in the first place.

Scratch that.

He'd have their balls for not immediately returning to the base when they'd realized the main road had been compromised.

Chase walked slowly alongside the convoy, aware that his team had taken up defensive positions that would enable them to provide cover if fighting did break out. As he came around the front of the lead MRAP, he saw Elena crouched down in front of a child, speaking to him. Beside her, one of the soldiers translated. At least the guy had his rifle out and in his hands, Chase thought bitterly, and not slung across his back as if they were at a damned church social.

"Elena," he called.

She turned and saw him, and for just an instant there was no recognition in her eyes. Then she smiled, and the relief and sheer joy he saw on her face made him go a little weak.

"Elena, get in the truck," he said, keeping his voice low as he walked slowly toward them.

"What?" She looked bewildered, her gaze flying from the weapon he held in his hands, to the convoy where she must have been able to see his team drawing down on them, back to his face.

"What's going on?" she asked, but she obediently rose to her feet and took several steps back, away from the villagers. "This is Kadir. Remember Kadir?"

Chase let his gaze flicker to the child, and recognized the boy they had treated for a broken wrist. He sported a cast on one arm.

"Yeah," he answered. "I remember Kadir. Now do as I say and walk slowly toward me. This is not a safe situation."

ELENA HARDLY RECOGNIZED the hard-eyed man who stood there as the same man who had left her just ten days earlier. With his scruffy beard and dirty clothes, he looked more like an insurgent than he did a special ops soldier. The expression in his eyes was one of cold intent, and she realized that if any of the villagers made a misstep, he wouldn't hesitate to shoot first and ask questions later.

For the first time, she understood the risk she'd taken in leaving the MRAP. The soldiers had tried to prevent her from approaching the villagers, but she had recognized Kadir and had wanted to see for herself that the child was on the mend. Now she realized that she had put herself and the villagers in very real danger.

Before she could retreat gracefully, however, one of the village men pushed his way forward. Elena didn't miss how Chase's hand tightened on his weapon. The man was elderly, with a long beard and deep wrinkles, but his dark eyes were shrewd. Elena didn't need to be told that this man was quite possibly the tribal leader. He didn't acknowledge Elena, but directed his attention to the soldier who stood tightly coiled, ready to spring.

As the old man began to speak, Chase visibly relaxed and reluctantly lowered his weapon.

"He says that Kadir is his grandson," he translated, "and that he's grateful to the American soldiers for providing medical treatment for his injuries."

The old man bent down toward the boy and reached beneath the child's tunic, withdrawing the angel necklace. The tiny charm winked against his wizened palm as he continued talking.

"He assures us that the American soldiers will be granted safe passage through these territories," Chase continued, "and that no harm will come to the woman who showed such kindness to his family."

Chase's gaze flicked briefly to Elena, but his expression was shuttered. He said something in return to the elderly man, and then held out his hand to Elena. "Let's go," he said. "Now."

Elena allowed herself one last glance at Kadir, who stood watching wide-eyed, before making her way past Chase to the MRAPs. She heard the whirring of a helicopter, and looked up to see a Black Hawk pass overhead, a gunner clearly visible in the open doorway, and her chest tightened in dread.

She climbed inside the MRAP, fully expecting Chase to follow her. *He had come back safely.* But to her dismay, he stalked past the convoy of armored trucks and climbed into the Humvee with his men. The two soldiers who had been assigned to escort her climbed into the MRAP with her, and as they closed the pneumatic doors, Elena was bitterly aware that Chase didn't give her so much as a second glance.

He was furious with her, and she couldn't blame him. She had no business leaving the MRAP, but had never guessed she might be in any danger. When they had come upon the rockfall, her military escort had suggested they return to the base. She might have agreed if the other soldier hadn't mentioned the detour through the little village of Jani. She had wanted to visit the drilling site, and the detour had seemed like a safe option. She still wasn't certain what had happened back there, but sensed she had dodged a bullet, both literally and figuratively.

When they arrived at the motor pool, she waited impatiently for the soldiers to open the rear door of the MRAP, intent on intercepting Chase. But by the time she climbed out, the Humvee was empty and Chase and his men were nowhere in sight. Frustrated, she began walking toward the contracting center when a voice called her name. Pausing, she turned to see a second Humvee driving slowly toward her. As it drew alongside, she recognized the base commander, Colonel Vinson, in the driver's seat. He didn't look very happy.

"Ms. De la Vega," he said coolly. "I'm glad to see you...alive. Climb in, please," he commanded. "You and I are going to have a little chat about protocol and the rules of engagement."

Elena blew out a hard breath, knowing this was one bullet she wasn't going to dodge so easily.

Two weeks, Elena thought in dismay, as she made her way across the base to her living quarters. Her soon-to-be ex–living quarters. Two weeks was all she'd managed to last before she'd been given the heave-ho.

She hefted her flak vest over her arm and let her helmet dangle from her hand. If Chase could see her, he'd give her hell for not wearing her protective gear, but why bother? She almost hoped a mortar would squash her flat. God, she'd never felt so embarrassed or ashamed.

She recalled the conversation she'd had with Colonel Vinson in his office and cringed. Despite the fact that he'd been courteous and even kind, he'd made it clear that she had put both herself and his men in danger by leaving the safety of the MRAP. Worse, he'd suggested that the soldiers who'd made the decision to detour through the village of Jani, rather than return to the base, might receive a reprimand for their actions. Elena had tried to explain that she was to blame, not them; she'd been determined to visit the drilling site and prove that she could do her job.

She swiped angrily at her damp cheeks. She'd known that taking the detour was a foolish decision, but had she cared? No. She'd actually encouraged the soldiers to ignore protocol and do whatever it took to get her to the drilling site. And they had, because they'd been young and stupid and had wanted desperately to impress her. If she'd been a man, they probably would have held their ground and insisted on returning to the base. But because of her misguided priorities, she'd nearly gotten them all killed.

Colonel Vinson had explained to her, in excruciating detail, about the planned ambush. She'd been shocked, and then horrified by her own role in the morning's events. No wonder Chase hadn't wanted to see her. He must be as disgusted with her as she was with herself. But the colonel hadn't seemed angry with her. In fact, if she hadn't known better, she'd have thought he was actually amused. He'd told her that while she had disregarded protocol by leaving the MRAP, he credited her with actually averting a firefight as a result of her kindness to a little boy. He'd gone on to suggest that he was doing her a favor by sending her away. As if leaving Sharlana—and Chase—was some kind of reward.

No doubt Chase would be thrilled to hear that she was leaving. Her heart clenched painfully at the knowledge that she wouldn't see him again. She would board a helicopter in the morning that would take her to Bagram Air Base, where she would work for the remainder of her six-month deployment. Bagram wasn't that far from Sharlana, but it might as well have been on the other side of the world.

Colonel Vinson was right; she should be thrilled with the relocation. Two weeks ago, she would have been. Bagram Air Base was known for its amenities, including an indoor swimming pool and an ice-skating rink. As far as recreation and support services went, the base was second only to the Green Zone in Baghdad. She'd have her own small apartment and access to a state-of-the art fitness center. She should be delighted.

She wanted to cry.

Just the thought of leaving Chase, of never seeing him again, made her inexplicably depressed. She could care less where they assigned her because without Chase, none of it mattered.

She opened the door to her living quarters and dropped her vest and helmet unceremoniously onto the floor.

"I thought we agreed you would wear your protective gear whenever you left your quarters," drawled a deep voice.

Elena spun around. Chase leaned negligently in the doorway to her bedroom. He had showered and shaved, and wore a black T-shirt and a pair of clean camo pants.

His face was leaner than she remembered, and sunburned, but his hazel eyes glowed as he watched her. A tornado of emotions whirled through her.

"Chase." His name came out on a croak. "What are you doing here? I got the distinct feeling you were avoiding me."

"Damn straight I was avoiding you. Hell, I practically sprinted from the motor pool to avoid seeing you." He grinned, his teeth startling white in his tanned face.

Elena stepped over her vest and approached him, drinking in the sight of him. Alive. Vital. She wanted to touch him and reassure herself that he was really there. But something was so not right with this picture.

"If you didn't want to see me, then why are you here?" she asked carefully.

"Correction," he said, shoving his hands into his pockets. "I didn't want *you* to see *me* when I looked like an animal and smelled like a goat. Especially not when I couldn't trust myself around you."

A tiny bud of hope bloomed in Elena's chest.

"Is that why you didn't ride back with me in the MRAP?" she asked. "Because you couldn't trust yourself?"

He gave a huff of laughter. "I couldn't trust myself not to shake the living hell out of you." He pulled his hands out of his pockets and straightened. "Jesus, Elena, what the hell were you thinking to do something so stupid?"

The bud of hope shriveled and curled in on itself, and Elena covered her face with her hands and turned away. "I don't know!" she cried, not able to face his censure. "I didn't think there would be any harm in taking the detour, and then I saw little Kadir by the side of the road, and I just wanted to make sure he was okay. I'm sorry. I screwed up!"

"Elena, don't cry," he groaned, and then she was in his arms. "Please don't cry, babe."

And then, amazingly, he was kissing her as if he couldn't get enough of her, his hands roaming over her body and burying themselves in her hair, tilting her face so that he could deepen the kiss, sweeping his tongue past her teeth and devouring her. Elena clung to him, kissing him back with her entire heart and soul.

When he finally pulled away, they were both breathing hard. Chase tipped his forehead to hers.

"I thought I was going to lose you," he said, and his voice cracked.

Elena smoothed her palms over his freshly shaven cheeks, cradling his face. "I'm leaving Sharlana. Tomorrow morning."

Chase turned his face into her palm. "I know."

"What?" Elena frowned, not understanding.

"Whose idea do you think it was to have you transferred?"

Elena gasped and snatched her hands away. She stared at him. "You? I'm losing my job because of you?"

"Elena—" He tried to catch her hands, but she held them up, warding him off.

"What right do you have, Chase?" Her voice was incredulous. "I know you think I can't take care of myself, and that women have no place in your dangerous world, but this is my job, Chase. My job, and my choice. Not yours."

God. She didn't want to leave Chase, but she didn't want him thinking that she was some kind of wimp who couldn't handle life on a forward operating base.

"I'm going to Bagram, too," he said quietly. "My team is being transferred, and I couldn't leave you here, Elena. Please understand."

She swallowed hard. "But you still think I need you to protect me, right?"

"I think you do just fine on your own," Chase smiled. "If it weren't for you—and your little guardian angel—those men might have been killed today."

Elena grimaced. "You don't have to be so nice to me, Chase. I was the reason those men took that detour."

Chase made a sound of frustration. "If it wasn't for you, that ambush would have killed the next bunch of guys who drove through that village. You prevented that, Elena. You did more to win the hearts and minds of the local people in just two weeks than the men on this base have been able to accomplish in two years. Do you get how huge that is?"

"Really?" Elena glanced at him. "So you don't think I'm a distraction to the men, and that I have no business being on a forward operating base?"

He searched her eyes. "I think you're a serious distraction, both to my heart and my peace of mind. Because of you, I've become exactly the kind of soldier I used to condemn."

"What kind of soldier is that?" she asked, needing to hear him say it.

"The kind who puts the safety and well-being of the woman he loves above everything else."

He loved her! Elena felt her heart swell until she was certain it would explode out of her chest.

Chase drew her close. "You've changed me, Elena. And while I know you'd do fine here at Sharlana for the next six months, I won't be fine at Bagram without you.

Besides, I think the other guys are onto us." He smoothed his thumb over her cheek. "I need you, Elena, and if that makes me weak, then so be it."

Elena laughed, her fingers closing reflexively over his muscled arms. "*Weak* isn't exactly the word that comes to mind when I think of you."

He tipped his head down to look at her. "And it's not the word I'd use to describe you, either. You're one of the strongest, most passionate women I've ever known. Please say you'll come to Bagram. My team and I will be based there for the next year. We'd have more opportunities to spend time together, and it's a big enough base that we wouldn't be under a microscope."

""Do I have a choice?"

"You always have a choice, Elena."

"What happens when my six months are up and I have to return to the States? Will you stay at Bagram?"

"Yeah, but I'll have two weeks of home leave that I can take, maybe more. I know you'll want to spend time with your family, but I thought maybe we could take a week and—"

"Yes," Elena interrupted.

"Yes?" Chase laughed. "You didn't let me finish. I was going to say that we could take a week and check into a romantic, oceanfront hotel somewhere. Sort of load up on what we'll need to make it through the last six months of my deployment. That is, if you're interested."

"Six months apart?" To Elena, it sounded like an eternity. How was she going to get through six months without Chase?

"I know it sounds like a long time, but it'll go by quickly," Chase assured her. "I'll call you as often as I can, and I'll have access to e-mail. I know we can make this work."

"Or I could extend my own deployment."

Chase leaned back to look at her, and Elena could see the flare of hope in his eyes that he quickly hid. "I wouldn't ask you to do that, Elena. I'd consider myself lucky just to have you at Bagram for the next six months."

Elena smiled, wreathing her arms around his neck. "I don't know...six months at Bagram? My life was pretty boring before I came to Sharlana. I mean, where else can a girl experience giant spiders, sandstorms, mortar attacks, close encounters with Taliban insurgents and the most incredible, amazing sex of her life?" She arched an eyebrow and gave Chase a challenging look. "How can Bagram possibly compare to that?"

Chase grinned and drew her closer. "I can't promise you that there won't be any sandstorms, but I can assure you that you'll be safe from spiders, mortar attacks and Taliban insurgents. As for the sex, keeping it incredible and amazing won't be a problem, I promise." He lowered his mouth to hers. "Let me show you."

Epilogue

North Carolina, one year later

ELENA STOOD by the baggage-claim carousel at Raleigh-Durham Airport and watched the passengers as they came through the security doors. She sucked in a deep breath, willing her nerves to calm down. She was a bundle of anticipation and anxiety, and it was all she could do to stand calmly and wait. She'd been waiting for three months, and now she just wanted to move on with her life.

She'd extended her deployment at Bagram by three months, both to spend more time with Chase and because she'd genuinely enjoyed the work she'd done there. After nine months together, leaving him in Afghanistan had been one of the hardest things she'd ever done. But she'd had work to do back in the States, too. Things she'd needed to take care of before Chase returned.

The security doors swung open, and suddenly there he was. Elena stopped breathing. He didn't immediately see her, and she took the opportunity to drink in the sight of him. He wore his desert camo uniform, and he looked lean and dangerous and altogether delicious. Then he

looked across the crowded terminal and saw her, and
Elena was struck again by how gorgeous he was. He
shouldered his way through the crowd, his eyes fastened
on her, until finally she was in his arms and he was kissing her with all the pent-up passion and frustration of
three long months apart. When he finally pulled back,
they were both breathless.

"What are you doing here?" he demanded, his voice
filled with amazement. His eyes devoured her as if he
couldn't believe she was really there, and his hands
stroked up and down her arms. "I wasn't expecting this.
I was going to fly up to D.C. this weekend to surprise
you."

Elena grinned foolishly at him. "Now you don't have
to. I don't live in D.C. anymore. I live here."

His expression turned into one of astonishment. "You
what?"

"I sold my condo and moved down here about a month
ago. I rented a little apartment in Morehead City. I've
been interviewing for a job at the contracting center at
Fort Bragg, and it's beginning to look like they might
make me an offer."

"You're going to be working at Fort Bragg?" His tone
was incredulous.

"It's a lot closer to Camp Lejeune than D.C., and…
well, let's just say I really needed a change."

Chase stared at her for a moment, and then he began
to laugh. Elena studied him uncertainly.

"You don't mind, do you?"

Chase hauled her against his chest and buried his face
in her neck. "No," he said roughly against her skin, "I
don't mind at all. I've been considering my options and
trying to figure out how we could be together. You just

solved that problem for me. How long is the lease on that apartment?"

Elena leaned back in his arms and searched his eyes. "Why do you ask?"

"Because I have a little house on the water near Camp Lejeune, and I think you'd really like it."

"Are you asking me to move in with you?"

"Lady," he growled, "since you left Bagram, the only thing I've thought about is how much I was looking forward to getting you alone for a solid month."

"Only a month?" she teased.

"That'll do for starters," he replied. "And four weeks is how much free time I have before I need to report back for duty."

"You're serious."

"Absolutely. I said I'd do whatever it takes to make this thing work, and I meant it. But I never guessed that you'd leave your job...your family..." He looked a little dazed.

"I'll do whatever it takes, too, Chase. We have something special, and I won't risk losing that." She cupped his face in her hands. "And if it means stepping out of my comfort zone and taking chances, then I'm willing to do that."

Standing on tiptoe, she kissed him, a moist, sweet fusing of their mouths that left her trembling with need.

"Christ," Chase said against her lips, "I've missed you so much. I've been thinking, too, that if we're going to make this work then I can't be disappearing from your life for months at a time."

"What do you mean?"

"I mean that I don't intend to do any more deployments. I'm going to request a transfer to the Marine

Special Operations School as an instructor. I was invited
to do that when I returned from Iraq, and I declined. But
things have changed. *I've* changed."

Elena caught her breath. "Are you sure?"

"Absolutely. Now let's get out of here and go home.
We have a lot of catching up to do, if you get my meaning."

She did.

And nothing had ever sounded so perfect.

* * * * *

COMING NEXT MONTH

Available September 28, 2010

REQUEST YOUR FREE BOOKS!

2 FREE NOVELS PLUS 2 FREE GIFTS!

HARLEQUIN®

Blaze

Red-hot reads!

YES! Please send me 2 FREE Harlequin® Blaze™ novels and my 2 FREE gifts (gifts are worth about $10). After receiving them, if I don't wish to receive any more books, I can return the shipping statement marked "cancel." If I don't cancel, I will receive 6 brand-new novels every month and be billed just $4.24 per book in the U.S. or $4.71 per book in Canada. That's a saving of at least 15% off the cover price. It's quite a bargain. Shipping and handling is just 50¢ per book.* I understand that accepting the 2 free books and gifts places me under no obligation to buy anything. I can always return a shipment and cancel at any time. Even if I never buy another book, the two free books and gifts are mine to keep forever.

151/351 HDN E5LS

Name _____ (PLEASE PRINT) _____

Address _____ Apt. #

City _____ State/Prov. _____ Zip/Postal Code

Signature (if under 18, a parent or guardian must sign)

Mail to the Harlequin Reader Service:
IN U.S.A.: P.O. Box 1867, Buffalo, NY 14240-1867
IN CANADA: P.O. Box 609, Fort Erie, Ontario L2A 5X3

Not valid for current subscribers to Harlequin Blaze books.

Want to try two free books from another line?
Call 1-800-873-8635 or visit www.morefreebooks.com.

* Terms and prices subject to change without notice. Prices do not include applicable taxes. N.Y. residents add applicable sales tax. Canadian residents will be charged applicable provincial taxes and GST. Offer not valid in Quebec. This offer is limited to one order per household. All orders subject to approval. Credit or debit balances in a customer's account(s) may be offset by any other outstanding balance owed by or to the customer. Please allow 4 to 6 weeks for delivery. Offer available while quantities last.

Your Privacy: Harlequin Books is committed to protecting your privacy. Our Privacy Policy is available online at www.eHarlequin.com or upon request from the Reader Service. From time to time we make our lists of customers available to reputable third parties who may have a product or service of interest to you. If you would prefer we not share your name and address, please check here. ☐

Help us get it right—We strive for accurate, respectful and relevant communications. To clarify or modify your communication preferences, visit us at www.ReaderService.com/consumerchoice.

HB10R

HARLEQUIN®

A Romance

FOR EVERY MOOD™

Spotlight on

Inspirational

Wholesome romances
that touch the heart and soul.

See the next page
to enjoy a sneak peek from
the Love Inspired® inspirational series.

See below for a sneak peek at
our inspirational line, Love Inspired®.
Introducing HIS HOLIDAY BRIDE
by bestselling author Jillian Hart

Autumn Granger gave her horse rein to slide toward the town's new sheriff.

"Hey, there." The man in a brand-new Stetson, black T-shirt, jeans and riding boots held up a hand in greeting. He stepped away from his four-wheel drive with "Sheriff" in black on the doors and waded through the grasses. "I'm new around here."

"I'm Autumn Granger."

"Nice to meet you, Miss Granger. I'm Ford Sherman, from Chicago." He knuckled back his hat, revealing the most handsome face she'd ever seen. Big blue eyes contrasted with his sun-tanned complexion.

"I'm guessing you haven't seen much open land. Out here, you've got to keep an eye on cows or they're going to tear your vehicle apart."

"What?" He whipped around. Sure enough, mammoth black-and-white creatures had started to gnaw on his four-wheel drive. They clustered like a mob, mouths and tongues and teeth bent on destruction. One cow tried to pry the wiper off the windshield, another chewed on the side mirror. Several leaned through the open window, licking the seats.

"Move along, little dogie." He didn't know the first thing about cattle.

The entire herd swiveled their heads to study him curiously. Not a single hoof shifted. The animals soon returned to chewing, licking, digging through his possessions.

Autumn laughed, a warm and wonderful sound. "Thanks,

I needed that." She then pulled a bag from behind her saddle and waved it at the cows. "Look what I have, guys. Cookies."

Cows swung in her direction, and dozens of liquid brown eyes brightened with cookie hopes. As she circled the car, the cattle bounded after her. The earth shook with the force of their powerful hooves.

"Next time, you're on your own, city boy." She tipped her hat. The cowgirl stayed on his mind, the sweetest thing he had ever seen.

*Will Ford be able to stick it out in the country
to find out more about Autumn?
Find out in HIS HOLIDAY BRIDE
by bestselling author Jillian Hart,
available in October 2010
only from Love Inspired®.*